The Butte

The Butterfly Lady

Danny M. Hoey, Jr.

Flaming Giblet Press
an imprint of Sundress Publications

Cover Art: *Untitled* by Stevie Walker-Webb

Book and Cover Design: T.A. Noonan

Series Editor: T.A. Noonan

Copy Editor: Adam Nicholson

Colophon: The primary font in this book is Didot, with additional elements in Helvetica and Edmondsans Regular. Didot and Lavanderia were used on the cover, with additional elements in Type Embellishments One LET and Helvetica. The "fG" Flaming Giblet Press logo is a combination of Lavanderia and Bebas Neue fonts.

Flaming Giblet Press is an imprint of Sundress Publications specializing in prose, cross-genre, experimental, and/or otherwise unclassifiable texts.

http://www.sundresspublications.com/fgp

For my mother, Sharon Hoey, who showed me the beauty of words.

If I didn't define myself for myself, I would be crunched into other people's fantasies for me and eaten alive.

—Audre Lorde

Music is your own experience, your own thoughts, your own wisdom. If you don't live it, it won't come out of your horn.

—Charlie Parker

He slit the throat of the man called the Butterfly Lady. Then, in handwriting as neat and clean as a third-grade teacher's, Chance Armstrong wrote: *I wanted a father. He made him leave. I am sorry.*

He took the paper and placed it on the vanity that held a picture of a young woman with a black hat on her head that covered her left eye. The boy used the linen cloth that still lay folded in the lap of the Butterfly Lady to clean the knife that he used, stuck the knife into his back pants pocket, and walked out the door. When Virginia, the boy's always-dreaming mother, walked across the hall and found and read the note that laid out the reason, she stuffed it in her mouth to stifle the scream that clawed at her throat— not because of the crime itself, but because the *him* that left she craved also.

It was July 1983 in Cleveland, Ohio, and as people watched the morgue roll out the body whose slender wrist jutted from under the black covering, slips of memory about the little black girl found on 55th and Woodland resurfaced: her right leg tucked neatly under her left leg like a baby doll, her eyelids stitched closed. They faintly remembered the stench of blood that wafted through their open windows from the '66 Hough Riots, images of flaming bodies roamed periodically in their night dreams. But the memory of this death would go away completely, evaporate into the nothingness that his life had been to them. No one would come out and say that they were glad that he was gone. But what their mouths wouldn't say their bodies did: they reassured each other—men reached for women in sundresses and Capri pants that they learned to ignore years ago, women held on tightly with the tips of their fingers to forgotten children made more important by the body stretched under the blackness. They were comforted with the understanding that there would be no investigation, no questions asked. No. It was a black man in a dress. Dead. Long ago dead to a world that turned off its light to him years before they stood, with slight satisfaction, and watched his body rolled out. However, if anyone had asked, or cared enough to know about the man called the Butterfly Lady, Chance Armstrong could have told them.

But they didn't.

1

She stared out of the store window, Mrs. Lee, and swept at nothing. Outside, loud voices argued in three-part harmonies, their arms punctuating the air like seasoned choir directors. Lean, black bodies moved like prizefighters, waiting for the *ding ding ding* of the bell— their bravado at the heart of the argument. Lee's Grocery and Beverage sat on the corner of 127th and St. Clair Avenue, sandwiched between the too-quiet Methodist church and the Quick-Fast Dry Cleaners. Above the store were two apartments separated by a small square of faded blue carpet; green paint curled away from the walls like lemon peels. Across the street was a skating rink, its sidewalk littered with kids in cut-off jean shorts, white T-shirts, and unlaced PRO-Keds; their eyes aching for, then disappointed by, the sign that promised—good times on wheels—but never opened. Next to the rink was an empty parking lot with a black and gold Chevy Impala sitting on cinder blocks. In this heat, the asphalt shimmered like wet skin. A barefoot homeless man in a purple sweater and black corduroys carried a brown paper bag filled to the brim with crushed aluminum cans. He tried to interrupt the harmonizing men, standing in-between the ones on tippy-toe, but was run off before he could.

The neighborhood was bereft of green—the trees, ancient and unmoving, shed bark like dried skin. The concrete sagged in certain spots and those not careful could lose a shoe or turn an ankle. Mrs. Lee looked back at Gabriel, the softness and sharp angles of his face startling, and swept to the chorus of the black men: each note, each chord reminded her of the difficulties of living in a place with no green and disappointment. She sighed heavily and gripped the broom harder. "Did you sell that boy cigarettes?" She stopped the broom in mid-air.

"You know I did, and his name is Chance." Gabriel stopped flipping through *Vogue* magazine and used his index finger as a placeholder.

"Why can't she come down and get them herself?"

"You know why, honey. She wrapped up in that man of hers."

"Oh, yeah?"

"Yes, ma'am. I heard them fighting a few days ago, and I told Chance to come over until it was over. It's a shame."

"You need to mind your own business."

"He is my business. Been my business since the day Virginia's water broke all over my pumps."

"I say leave it alone. Don't stick your nose where it won't fit. And he isn't yours."

"Somebody needs to act like he theirs."

"You see anything good in there?" Lee pointed to the magazine as she walked toward the cooler nearest the door. She leaned the broom against it, pulled out a carton of Neapolitan ice cream, and looked at its expiration date.

"Everything...but nothing I can afford."

"Well then, get back to counting that drawer, and when you are done, I need you to move those boxes of pork and beans to the top shelf."

"That will make me sweat. I have to have my face on at all times!"

"Your face? Ha! I need you to move pork and beans. Not go to a Hollywood premiere. And from what I can remember, Hollywood hasn't once knocked on your door."

"Don't I look good, though?" Gabriel took his hands and framed his face and extended his neck.

"You look silly," Lee said as she bolted the front door. "Don't you get tired of wearing that gook?"

"I am who I am." Gabriel came from behind the counter, stopped in front of Lee and did a half turn. "The things I used to do with these."

"Take it off."

"If I did that, I would scare away the customers."

"They will come. I'm not worried about them."

They always came. Gabriel knew this. They had come since he started working in Lee's in 1970—to see him. Gabriel came to work dressed in pieces he learned to make on his own: silk scarves that covered his angular head when he didn't feel up to a wig, long shirts that draped at the sleeve swallowing his already thin arms, anything short (the weather didn't matter) or tight that highlighted the legs that he had become famous for.

Gabriel was six feet tall and the color of pennies, and there was a beauty hidden beneath the layers of makeup he applied to his face each morning. No one knew what he looked like under there, except for Lee, and it didn't matter to them—Gabriel's *"don't do me, Miss Thing, or I won't be worth a nickel"* or *"don't come for me unless I send for you"* did it for the customers as much as just the sight of him. Some thought he looked like a celebrity, someone they thought they saw on some old-time television show, the way his arms flourished when he talked, the way he pulled them in with the large, expressive, painted-on eyebrows. Others thought he was a show just for them, in their honor— simple amusement to take their minds off the daily disappointments they faced as they went through the humdrum of their lives. A way to exercise mediocrity, the slight but sharp pains of rejection experienced and internalized, daily. Either way they looked at it, it was something that they had come to expect on their weekly shopping trips—some picked up soda crackers bent over in laughter, others held loaves of Wonder Bread while they wiped tears from their eyes. Others fingered boxes of baking powder for cornbread with smiles on their faces, secretly wishing that something would drop from the sky and stop all of the madness. They all came to erase, if only temporarily, some type of hurt and to see the spectacle that Gabriel had become…

Mrs. Lee picked up the broom. "How long have you been here? I rarely see you without makeup. You look like a clown."

"A clown, Miss Thing?"

"This is America. You have democracy. You can be who you want to be. Stop hiding."

"Democracy? A white woman wearing two-hundred-dollar pumps in a white fur coat in the middle of summer, that's democracy. A white man in Washington arguing to make his pockets bigger, that's democracy. But a black man? A black man in Washington fighting for his rights is a crime, an affront against the white man's soul. A black man in a dress? Now that's a shame because white men love it and want to hide the fact that they do, and black people despise it and try their best not to claim it, to run as far away from it as they can. Then, when they can't hide from it or when it's in the very place they say can't be touched or broken, they create this rope called Jesus and hang you with it. My neck is sore. Why hide? It's not hiding—it's survival."

"What are you surviving from? You don't go anywhere but to the store and up to your apartment. Who are you surviving against? I don't get it. You people have all the opportunity in the world and you waste it. Me?" Lee stopped sweeping and stared at Gabriel. She wore a skirt the color of rosemary, a short-sleeved yellow shirt with a Calla lily in the center; her silver hair was in two tight braids—the part split her face in half. "Me, I had to fight for this store, you know. You don't know what it means to survive." In Mrs. Lee's mind, she was a survivor. She lived through a loveless marriage, not being able to have kids, and folks who didn't think a woman should own a store or be in charge of her entire person.

"So they making you struggle for a little piece of the pie? So what? What do you think it says about folks like me who couldn't get a loan for a milkshake? This country ain't made for people like me. I'm just living in it best I can." Gabriel did a slow pirouette, extended his right leg, and walked tippy-toe to the counter.

"Stop all that ballerina mess and count my money." Lee smiled at him and continued to sweep. "I'm an old woman. I need all the rest I can get."

After he finished counting the drawer, Gabriel left the store and went up the back stairs to his apartment. He walked straight to the kitchen. Gabriel poured Riesling into a mason jar, stood in the kitchen doorway and looked around the apartment. It was bare except for a Victrola, a four-post bed with a red and green bedspread, an unfinished rocking chair that sat across from the bed, and a blondwood vanity table that was framed with light bulbs. In the top left-hand corner of the vanity was a faded picture of his mother Mattie in a blue dress with a black hat that covered the left side of her face. Gabriel walked to the vanity, sat down at it, and looked at his mother. He rubbed the legs that killed her. They were thinner now, but still strong. Back then, his legs were muscular with calves like mountaintops. On the day of his mother's death, she saw Gabriel in full makeup, a long blond wig, and a butterfly headband that danced when he did, doing scissor kicks to "God Bless America," a performance that made his mother's head spin so hard that she went home on that oppressive summer day in July, got in bed, and never got up.

His father, Amos Smith—a Deacon not yet fire-baptized—told him that he killed his mother with wigs and *those* legs. Gabriel didn't stay around to see his mother buried, and as he boarded the Greyhound from Pittsburgh to Cleveland, Ohio, he clutched the picture of his mother with "God Bless America" still playing in his head.

Now he sat and stared at her picture, the black hat hiding parts of her from him. Some nights, he could remember her. Some nights she was nothing more than fuzz that floated on his brain. On the nights that he could remember her, he could see himself watching her as she sat at her vanity, putting on makeup. Her fingers like tiny paintbrushes, gently stroking her skin. He would try to get in her lap then, and she would hold him away telling him that she had to get "pretty for daddy." Her jet-black hair laid straight down her shoulders, shining in the light of the vanity bulbs, her eyes floating in the bright blue of her eyelids.

When he was ten, Gabriel was pretending that he was his mother when he was slapped across the room by hands that had to play with themselves in order not to kill him. His father, Amos—a Deacon not yet fire-baptized—caught him, and by the time his father slapped him, Gabriel had highlighted his eyes with electric-blue shadow and covered his lips with bright red lipstick. Then, he didn't know what a sissy was, but when his father dragged him from the spot where he landed down to his room, Gabriel had been called a "filthy little sissy boy" enough times to know that it was wrong.

"What the hell is wrong with you, boy?" Amos said as he stood over his son. "You want to make me look bad? You want God to punish me for letting you be a sissy?"

Gabriel lowered his head afraid that he would get hit again and mumbled, "I'm sorry."

"Sorry? Don't tell me sorry. Tell God sorry. Tell him that you don't...don't want to be a sissy. Tell him that your father was good to you and that you did this on your own." And suddenly, as if Amos had seen the lipstick for the first time, the heavily painted eyes, rouge on skin too soft, too smooth for a boy, his rage grew more, and he hit Gabriel on top of his head with the palm of his hand. Amos's breathing got louder, quicker; a sound slipped out of Amos's throat that startled him. His eyes darted around the room as if he suddenly realized that he was being watched: Amos had failed again, he thought. He had failed God once again and once again he was being punished.

Amos looked back at his son and grabbed his face. "I want to you to take this off. Take it off Gabriel, take it off take it off take it off." Amos held Gabriel's face in a grip that made him cry. "I'm not raising no filthy sissy, you hear me? I'm not doing it, and God as my witness, I'm not doing it." Amos looked to the ceiling and said it louder, "I'm not, God. I'm not!" Amos let Gabriel's face go then pinned him to the ground. "If I have to hold you here for the rest of your life, you will beg God to save you son, you will beg him!" Sweat dripped down the sides of Amos's dark, oval face, and his shaking hand held his son's head to the wooden floor. "I'm not!"

Amos didn't know that she was there until he heard her voice. "Amos Smith! Take your hands off my child!" Mattie stood there, her skin like cream turned brown. Mattie reached for her son and pulled him into her arms. She rubbed his head and stared at Amos—her eyes like hot embers. "What is wrong with you?"

"Me? What is wrong with me?" Amos paced back and forth in front of Mattie. "Look at him, Mattie. Look. You don't think this is wrong?"

Mattie looked down at Gabriel and sucked in air as the blue eye shadow ran down his face. She looked back up, past Amos, past the window, past the trees that shielded the front of their two-story house from the sun's torturous rays. She looked to see if there was an answer: was it her fault? Did she make Gabriel this way? He was her sugar lump. Her strong little teddy bear... Did she love him too much? Mattie sighed heavily and looked at Amos. "You need to go and clean yourself up. We still have church."

Amos stopped pacing and held his hands out to her, confused. "This is the problem. You let him sit up under you all day when he should be outside, riding a bike, tossing a ball, something, Mattie. Something other than sitting watching you at that fuckin' vanity."

"Watch it, Amos. We still serve the Lord around here." She turned her eyes up at him and he shook his head.

"I can't have this, Mattie. I can't. I'm already under fire, woman... If they found out...then I am ruined, you hear me, ruined. What has gotten into him, Mattie? Huh? Tell me, will you?"

Mattie pulled Gabriel closer and pointed toward the door. "Go. Let me deal with this." Before Amos walked away, she reached for Amos's hand. Her grip tightened, then she leaned in and whispered, "Amos, don't ever put your hands on my child again."

Amos shook his head some more and muttered, "I'm not," as he walked out of the bedroom.

Mattie took her son and sat him on the bed. She went to the hall closet, pulled out a rag, went into the bathroom and wet it. When she came back, she stopped in front of Gabriel and thought about the Bye and Bye. "Jesus," she whispered as she bent down and started to wipe the eye shadow and bright red lipstick from his face.

"Daddy loves you... You know that, right, Gabriel?"

Gabriel shook his head without picking it up.

"Pick your head up, boy. He just wants what's best for you." Mattie rubbed his lips with the now damp towel and let her fingers linger on his cheek. "Little boys don't wear lipstick or eye shadow. Did you know that, Gabriel?"

He shook his head no.

"Well, baby, they don't, so you have to be a big boy for me and not put on any more of my lipstick, you hear? We can't anger God, and he would be angry if you tried to look like me. Okay, Gabriel?" She wiped the rest of the lipstick off his lips and held the rag in her hand. "Now, go put on your suit for church."

By the time he turned thirteen, Gabriel's father's distance had become bearable — it was a preoccupation that was beyond Gabriel, beyond family — but his mother's refusal to spend time with him hurt worse than the whipping he got almost daily from the neighborhood bullies, Smokey and Bone. Mattie did what motherly duties she could do that didn't require her son to sit up under her — washed and folded his clothes, cooked meals but didn't sit at the table with him, fixed lunches and placed them in brown paper bags. When Gabriel would find her sitting in the front room next to the single-light lamp reading the Bible, he would sit at her feet. He was never sure if she was surprised or angry, but every time she would get up without saying a word and walk to another room.

Sitting alone after the times that his mother left didn't make him love her less. What it did was teach him that he didn't necessarily need love, but he did need attention. That he needed someone to look at him and acknowledge that he still existed. And since he wasn't getting it from home and since the only attention that the boys he grew up with gave him was violent and negative, he found some solace, if only temporary, in Ella Bagwell.

"Why you hang around me all the time?" Ella, brown-skinned and thin as a sheet of paper, sat in front of a large mirror.

"Why not?" Gabriel watched her intensely as she lit a match, blew it out, and traced her eyebrows. It had been years since his father tried to stomp his head into the ground, and seeing her apply the burnt end of a match to her face made the memory fresh.

"You are a boy. You're always in my room, and you never look at my tits." Ella laughed then stopped to put on plum-colored lipstick. She then traced her lips with a black eyeliner pencil and drew a dark line that followed the curve of her already full lips.

Gabriel grabbed her hands to stop her as she tried to trace her lips again. "That's too much. You want to accent the lips, not look like a fool."

"What you know about makeup?"

"Enough." He rolled the pencil in between his thumb and index finger as if he had discovered it for the first time.

"Shit. I always knew you were a fag."

"I'm not a fag. I just like the way women look made up."

"What you look like made up?" Ella stared at Gabriel, her eyes taking in the angular, penny-colored face, pouty lips she wanted badly, eyelashes that looked like silk wings. "Come here." Ella grabbed him and made him sit in front of the mirror.

Ella was a member of the Collinwood High School high-stepper team. The first and only black, and before every basketball game, she made her face up. Being the only black on the team, she was often booed when she did her high-kicks at games. Even though she was at the end of the line, her hand barely touching the white shoulder that flinched each time that she reached out for it, she kicked and smiled and figured that if she could get them to look at her face—see the time she took to enhance her beauty, look at the sincerity in her eyes—that they would learn to like her and keep whatever they felt for her skin inside until they made it to their homes.

Ella took out a pink compact with white lilies on it and flipped it open. She took out the powder puff, dabbed it against the pad, and began to apply it to Gabriel's face.

Gabriel moved his face from her soft fingers. "That's too light for me."

Ella smirked and grabbed his chin in her hand—the soft fingers turned steel. "A shade lighter makes your skin seem lighter. Every dark woman knows this. They won't look at you if you too dark." She finished applying the powder, let his chin go and watched with satisfaction as Gabriel turned from left to right.

"What you think?"

"It's still too light, and I don't have a hard time getting them to look at me." Gabriel took the puff and wiped at his right cheekbone where the powder seemed uneven. "Hell, they all look at me. They call at me. Men. They grab their dicks and follow me home." Gabriel looked through a purple bag full of makeup and pulled out a ruby-red lipstick tube. He applied it, and the paint was so wet and bright that it looked like his lips were bleeding. "My father won't talk to me because he sees them looking at me when we walk down the street. I try not to look back, but I live in a house where I talk to myself, hold myself, look at myself. So, every once in a while, I look."

"Well..." Silence crept up in Ella's throat. She didn't know how to answer because the look on Gabriel's face made her suck back what she had intended to say. "I'll be right back." Ella left and when she came back she had a blond wig in her hands. "This is my mama's. She only wears it when she goes to Pearl's on Saturday night. Half the time, it makes it back to the house before she does, so she won't miss it." Ella put it on his head and stepped back.

"Hell, you're prettier than I am. No wonder they always

staring." Ella knew how much she hated herself and couldn't stand or deal with anyone who hated themselves more than she did.

"I don't know. My father would really kill me then. I would wake up to him stuffing the pages of the Bible down my throat." Gabriel broke into laughter at the thought of it and pinched his eyes shut to try and stop the tears.

"Stop all that mess. You gon' mess up your make-up. I thought you knew that." Ella's soft-then-steel hands rubbed his shoulders. She then moved away quickly and picked something up off her bed. "Here." Ella placed a headband with colorful butterflies with extended wings on his head. She stepped back and laughed. "Stand up."

Gabriel stood up. "I look silly, Ella."

"You look good. I bet you would look good in one of my minis. Legs to die for."

"I would really have to kill my daddy then."

Ella went to her closet and pulled out a red dress that looked like it was missing a bottom half. "Put this on."

Gabriel put the dress on and looked at himself in the mirror. In spite of the horror that spread in the bottom of his stomach, he smiled.

"Let's go."

"What? Man, you're crazy?"

"I have to be at the game soon. I'll tell them you're my cousin."

That was so long ago, and Gabriel sometimes wondered about Ella and whether or not she found that place that she was looking for. Did she find the right makeup to cover the scars she got while aching for acceptance? Would she ever be satisfied, he wondered, with the realization that the skin she was in was it—that it was the thing that defined her—made her who and what she was. Gabriel never saw her again but thought about her frequently. Her self-hatred he didn't understand then, but now he carried it like the pressed powder that absorbed in his skin.

Gabriel got up from the vanity and walked back to the kitchen. "Huh," he said out loud to himself as he poured another glass of Riesling. "What would God say now, Mama?" He opened his arms wide and bowed to the picture on the mirror. He took the bottle of wine and sat it beside the rocking chair. He slid down into the chair and rocked back and forth. He tried to think of her now and his brain was a little slower, fuzzier than it had been earlier. This was like those nights when he couldn't see her clearly. Those nights long after the street noise had died down when children, exhausted from teasing one another, found their way into their homes; when pimps reclined in 1976 Chevys, fingering the wads of folded money, and whores tiptoed to their pads because they found their main trick for the night and were unwilling to share. Those nights when nothing stirred, when the air was thick with the promise of rain, he missed her more, for he couldn't connect her to anything, couldn't pin down the moment when he lost her. She was like a lost memory on those nights: one that floats around freely, searching for its place, looking for the spot where it belonged, searching, until it gives up, unable to find its place to breathe, its place to live in this world, and it leaves, and makes the one unhappy who couldn't hold it down, couldn't wrap their fingers around it to love it, to inhale the delicious pleasure that it was sure to provide if it could find its way home.

Gabriel's head was beginning to get heavy, and he tried to rock faster. But the wine had taken over his body and he felt himself falling into the dream.

It is the same dream. He is there. Each night. Standing on the corner of a street that seems to have no end and no beginning. There is plenty of light on this street, and he can see buildings with pointy tops that seem to puncture the sky. He stands at this corner and wonders why it is so empty. Gabriel's clothes are the same as in the other dreams: black dress pants, a button-up bone-white shirt, wingtipped black shoes and a black felt hat with a strip of brown around its edges. He is clean, and he struts to there and nowhere. He walks to a laundromat that he can never recall the name of and stops and stares in its window. The dryers spin like kaleidoscopes full of bright colors: reds, blues, yellows, oranges, greens. And his eyes are transfixed for what feels like hours, hypnotized by the colors. Then he moves toward a building shaped like the front of a church, and she comes. Always comes: his mother. In a long, pale dress that covers her ankles, with long, white gloves that reach to her elbows and the black hat that he loves with the lace that hangs like a shadow on one side of her face.

She always walks—no, floats down the burnt stairs of the building shaped like the front of a church and holds her hand to him as if she is expecting him. He hurries, at once becoming a little kid again, in knee-length knickers, a green-and-white striped shirt, and a blue hat for boys. Once he reaches her, she takes his hand and they glide down the never-ending street. He smiles and holds her hand tightly. He tries to squeeze it hard to see if he can hold her forever, to see if it would hurt her. She lets him, never looking down, never saying a word. He squeezes and squeezes until he is a man, until he can see the dust from her bones falling into his hands. He can no longer feel his mother, her bone dust in his hands — her arm alive without her hand.

When she leaves, she is ahead of him, and he chases after her on the never-ending street and then she stops in front of a tall red building and she is still, silent. But floating, and he runs after her, past her as she stands at the tall red building and suddenly it is dark: the bright never-ending street losing itself to the night. He is alone. He is afraid and he sees her at the top of the tall red building. Then he reaches toward her, wanting to give her back her hand and there they stand. Men. Hundreds of men with distorted faces and red eyes that float in and out of their heads. Their mouths like harps and their arms long, with thick, sharp claws. One reaches for him and takes off his hat. Another cuts his left arm, the bone-white sleeve falling like confetti. He sees his blood falling to the ground and runs. He runs as fast as he can down the never-ending street but goes nowhere. He turns and they are next to him, shouting, *"Eat his skin!"* His arms hurt and his legs are tired and he is in an alley and he panics because he doesn't know how he got there. He looks around and sees his friends: Mrs. Lee, Virginia, Old Man, and he is calling to them only they look right past him with eyes as red as those chasing him.

Now he begins to cry. Begins to cry because they can't help him. Because he crushed his mother's hand to dust. He looks back at them and they stand and then their bodies start to sway and he feels a gush of wind and he falls forward and he is comforted for a moment because he thinks he is falling toward them. But when the wind stops, he is surrounded by red eyes and harps and claws that rip at his skin. They have him and he flails about and he screams for them to help him but they are still. When he looks back to the people holding him he is in front of the tall red building. He is kneeling in front of the tall red building. He is tired. His clothes are gone. He is naked and cold. He looks up, instantly shamed when he sees his mother's black-laced face staring at his nakedness. He tries to cover up but his hands are bound and he can only cry out in shame. The doors of the tall red building open and there is a man, seven feet tall, with a bible in his hand. The agony and the shame of being naked in front of his mother won't allow him to pay closer attention. In one leap, the seven-foot man is before Gabriel. His breath smells like garlic and vinegar and his red eyes shine like rubies from beneath the black robe that he wears. On the outside of each robed arm are white bands that sparkle like fresh fallen snow. Gabriel feels the breath of the seven-foot man and lifts his body up to his mother for help. The man kicks him, and Gabriel lands on his back, forced to look into the shiny ruby eyes. The man speaks:

"Why have you not confessed your sins?"

"Forgive me, for I have not sinned"

"You have sinned, my son. Why not confess?"

Gabriel tries to sit up, but when he does, sharp claws scratch at his skin.

"You are not pure," the man says as he pours liquid on Gabriel's naked black skin. *"It's simple. We have to tear you apart to make you whole again."*

Gabriel looks to his mother and pleads with her, then lowers his eyes. He looks up again, and he can only see the ground; he is upside-down, and claws are ripping into him. His mother kneels in prayer; her handless arm makes him wish that he hadn't crushed it. She starts to pray: *"Lord, if You can calm a raging sea, if You can calm the waters, rock me to sleep in these thunderous times. Lord, please set him free. Set him free, Lord."* And as she prays, Gabriel is torn in two: one side of him in her arms, the other in the claws.

2

Virginia Armstrong craved a box of Lemonheads. The sharp, tangy crunchiness of the candies calmed her nerves, and Virginia needed the candy after the argument that she had with LeRoi — her on-again-off-again man. She sent her son Chance downstairs to Lee's for a box and some Newports and wondered what was taking him so long. Virginia chewed the inside of her lip, her tongue running along the broken skin that substituted for the crunchy candies, and thought more about the fight. Virginia hated these moments, these spaces of time that separated her from LeRoi. They fought over the same thing: LeRoi's knack for disappearing for days, weeks, even months at a time. And then, as if he knew that Virginia was on the verge of madness, he would show up at her door, as if he only went to the corner store for milk and eggs. Virginia was lonely when LeRoi was gone, and having only her son to look at when he was gone was not enough. She didn't even like Chance.

Virginia leaned over the rail and ran her red-tipped nails through her hair. Frustrated, she called down in the direction of the store, "Chance?" No response. The only thing that she heard were the voices of the few people who walked past the store, knots of laughter fighting through serious tones. "I wish he hurry the hell up. My nerves are bad."

Virginia thought about going downstairs but didn't have the energy to deal with Gabriel. She hated to see him on that stool—the way he measured her with one look and summarily dismissed her with the same look caved her chest in at times. Every time Virginia saw him, he questioned her about LeRoi, about her need for him, about her inability to function without him. Standing in front of Gabriel during those moments, she just stared and ran her fingers through her hair. It was hard for Virginia to really explain what LeRoi did to *her*, so why try and explain it to someone else. Why try and explain to anyone, let alone Gabriel, that LeRoi's love gave her life order and clarity. That the way he sang to her calmed her anxious heart, allowed her to sleep better at night. Why tell anyone that the picture that she held in her coat pocket when she left her mother, her childhood, didn't matter when he was around; that the dullness that blunted her was eased, made more bearable. Why tell anyone that she waited on him because in her mind, her life depended on it—her words formed more easily when he was around; her eyes saw light when there was none to see... It was during the times that she was waiting that Virginia knew exactly what her mother was talking about when she was a young girl in Cincinnati,

Ohio.

"It grabs you and won't let go," Virginia's mother, Ruby, said to her aunt, Fan, on a sticky day in June 1963, as they sat in the kitchen of their walk-up home.

"I know what you mean." Fan, lean and tall and dark as a cocoa bean, sat across from her sister, shaking her head. During the day, they both worked as maids and tied their hair up. But now, Fan's black hair hit her neck like cool air.

The thing that held them, and what Virginia stood in the kitchen doorway to hear about every day, was the stories, *As The World Turns*, that they watched every day at 1:30 p.m. In the midst of mopping, cooking a dinner that they would never eat, washing laundry, sweeping porches, making and serving coffee, they managed to find time to watch a show that kept them reeling more than the eight children that they had between them. It also gave them an excuse, a reprieve of some sort, to slip in and out of the weariness and lackluster shine of their lives; the show bracketed and made their lives more bearable.

Ruby Armstrong, short and stocky, was the exact opposite of her sister: she had buttermilk skin and cropped black hair with streaks of gray that sparkled in kitchen light. Both of them worked hard as soon as they walked into the doors of their employers—unable to see their kids off to school—to have a half hour of peace from the world that shunned them because they were black and female.

"Did you see what Lisa did today?" Ruby picked up a bag of pinto beans, ripped a quarter-sized hole in the bag, and poured a handful into her palm.

"White people can do anything they want, Ruby. You

know that."

"She treats that little Tommy like he is a bug swarming around her food. Like swatting him to death wouldn't mean a thing."

"Lisa only used him to get Bob to stay. Tommy ain't never mattered, Ruby."

"That boy is going to grow up a stranger to his own mama."

They sat like this, Ruby and Fan: as if the people they talked about were real. As if they could touch them, grab them by the shoulders, and shake them for their blatant disregard for the good life they led.

"Virginia, hand me that bowl on the counter."

Virginia, sixteen, the color of roasted pecan shells, with large, oval eyes and lips that were slightly parted even when closed, walked to the counter while staring at the mouths of the women who talked about Lisa. Virginia was the oldest of her siblings and had to watch them when her mother was at work. Her mornings were spent stirring oatmeal, stuffing legs and arms in gently worn clothes, and walking kids to school. There weren't moments for her to think about her life or figure out the world and how it worked in the midst of lumpy oatmeal and too-small clothes. There weren't moments, or time for that matter, for her to realize who she was or how she should live—like the best way to wear her hair so that it complemented her face—long and straight with a black or blue barrette holding pieces of bang to the side of her head, or curly with a part straight down the middle. Or time to really appreciate how the length of her legs drove both boys *and* men crazy. There weren't spaces for these moments of reckoning, so she lived for the conversations at the table with her mother and aunt—they gave her some idea, some slice of what life was or what it could be... Bit by bit, she pieced together little parts of the lives that they spoke of, fretted over daily. Just the thought of what Lisa did—who she had fooled, who she had tricked into falling in love with her, what fancy clothes she had on—was enough to get Virginia through the wet, gummy hands that stuck to her as they walked each day to school. Turning down a spot in the double dutch line had become customary—listening to what Lisa did became necessary.

Virginia reached for the bowl, still looking at her mother holding the brown beans in her hands, and knocked it off the counter. The clanging sound of the metal made her mother and aunt look up at her.

"Lord, what is wrong with you today? Pick that bowl up and bring it to me."

"These children." Fan stood up and walked to the stove. Once bright white, it was now worn, coated in a thick film of grease with finger streaks down the sides; it only had two pilots that worked. "Which one of these works, Ruby? I'm too old to play eeny meeny miny moe!" Fan laughed and grabbed the kettle.

"The last two, Fan, and you know it. Don't be sly." Ruby looked up at Virginia. "Well, girl, what you gon' do? Hold the bowl hostage? Give it here." Ruby reached for the bowl and took it out of Virginia's hand. Ruby sat the bowl on the table and reached for her daughter. She rubbed her arm and smiled at Virginia. Ruby loved her. Loved Virginia more because she was first and because she was the one she could remember really holding on to. When Virginia was born, Carl Armstrong, Sr., was alive. He provided for them as a waiter at the Cincinnatian Hotel. And even though he wasn't making much money, it still allowed Ruby to stay home with her oldest and only child at the time. When Carl died, Ruby had Virginia, Wendy, and Carl, Jr., who was still nursing. Things changed drastically, and Ruby didn't know what it was like to leave her children for long periods. When she first started working as a maid with the Henrys, she would be sweeping, trying to remember if all of the children's faces showed that they were content, that they at least had enough food in their bellies to tide them over until she got home.

"Make your mama some coffee. Use what's left of the Folgers."

"Well, what you think about Lisa two-timing old Mr. Carter?"

"Two-timing? That man wanted her, and he would do anything for her. Shoot. Let me tell a man that I wanted some diamonds. He would look at me like I was half out my mind." Ruby picked the black marbles from the beans and sat them on a piece of newspaper; her fingers moved rapidly through the rest looking for any other deformities.

"See, on TV, them women can do that. You know?"

"Man, who you telling? Them women can do that *here*, Fan. Right where we living. They do it all the time. Just not us."

"Mr. Laurence came to me today and said that he was having trouble with the colored boys from up south." Fan heard the whistle from the kettle and before she could get up to get it, Virginia made it to the stove. Virginia went to the faded cabinet, grabbed two cups, put two teaspoons of Folgers and one teaspoon of powdered milk into them, poured boiling water, and placed the cups in front of her mother and aunt with the spoons still in them.

Ruby stirred her coffee and sat her spoon on the side. "Why he telling you?"

"Well, you know since King was on TV talking about a dream, Lord, the colored folks who came from Alabama, Memphis, Mississippi—cause that's what he gots working for him—folks from those places, they talking about a raise and being equal and he ain't trying to hear it." Fan sipped her coffee.

"Well, they can go on back south with that stuff." Ruby poured the last of the beans in her hand and looked at them carefully. She didn't raise her eyes and spoke low at first. "I have a dream, too. I want to feed my kids more than beans and fatback every day. I want to have a little cabbage and cornbread more often. I want to see my kids more, read some bedtime stories to them. But if they don't stop with all this 'we all free' and 'we want to be equal' stuff, it's going to ruin everything for all of us. I go to work, do what I have to do to get back, watch my stories without any worry, and come home to my kids. What else do I want?"

Ruby poured the beans into the silver bowl and watched them fall into the other beans like hard rain. She had seen rain today on *As The World Turns*, and it made her feel like a little girl again. Like she was five years old, sitting at her grandmother's feet, on an always-leaning porch. The rain always made her see clearer. It made her watch more closely, listen harder to the words that the white women who wore long dresses that hid their ankles said to them about God and his redemption—the fiery red-haired one stunning her deeper into silence. She listened to various white men in nice suits that came to collect dollar bills for insurance from her parents—suits she later saw and recognized when her boss wore them, suits she hung up in the closet still strangled by the plastic dry cleaner bags.

Ruby studied the men closer because they were speaking to her in a language that she slowly came to understand. Their words told her that she was a tiny, brown speck on the world that turned and shook everything—that she was on the outside looking in. They watched her world turned upside down on a daily basis while theirs stayed on track. The glue that kept her together she saw melt away while she stood outside their windows. They lived in turmoil for sure, but at the end there was always peace, always a glass of Jim Beam that made perfect ice cubes sizzle, a nice hot meal of meats that she had only prepared, a host of empty apologies. What they said brought a level of clarity to her: "I cannot be what you are therefore I cannot have what you have."

As Ruby listened to the backstory from the world—words that told her that she could not be them or could not have what they had—she became angry. Angry because she realized that there was nothing that she could do about it. She had kids to feed, and pinto beans and fatback were better than nothing; powdered milk would stretch and tasted better than water in cereal. She couldn't walk out the door, couldn't walk through the TV, join them, sit down at their tables and wrap her arms around Phillip, Mike, Paul, and say, "Lovely to see you." She couldn't taste the braised meat, the candied carrots, the garlic mashed potatoes, buttered dinner rolls. She couldn't swallow the Jim Beam, not choke on it, and enjoy it. No, she couldn't do any of that. Not at all, and so it was now clearer than ever that she couldn't hold her dream against theirs. And with this realization came an even more profound sense of reality that gnawed at an already fragile core. So at work, she let the lamb that she never cooked in her house fall on the floor, seasoned it, and put it on to broil; she used extra lye in the laundry and let it soak longer than usual, put more salt than sugar in the peach cobbler; she left the floors unswept and used the toothbrush to clean the floor tiles. As the years progressed, her anger had become complicated and edgy. "Let them tear up his place," Ruby said as she looked up at Fan. "Let him deal with it."

Virginia stood in the doorway and waited for them to finish talking about Lisa Hughes and how she won Mr. Carter over, not this thing of black men trying to get more money from white men. She shifted her weight from one foot to another, and when she realized that they weren't going to talk more about the woman who had become her hero, she went to her room.

In front of the mirror—the left corner edge missing— Virginia placed her hands on her hips, squinted her eyes like she imagined that Lisa would have, and made believe that she had the power to captivate men with just a look. Virginia tried walking across the room, like she imagined that Lisa would, and rubbed the side of her school dress.

There was no feeling of confidence, no level of freedom, nothing that assured her that what was outside of her world was hers for the taking. She swayed from side to side and tried to twirl strands of hair around her finger like she imagined that Lisa Hughes did. Nothing. She felt nothing, and nothing was different. Virginia let her hands fall from her hips and stared harder at herself in the mirror. All she saw was ordinary—black skin that didn't scream special; it didn't speak of promise. Legs that she thought were too long to be elegant, eyes too far apart on her face, the neck not long enough. Something had to change, and somehow she knew that it wouldn't happen because she hadn't been able to see Lisa Hughes for herself. Hadn't been able to see the magic that was Lisa Hughes.

A few months later, Virginia cut school to catch Lisa Hughes on the old black-and-white that they had in their front room. That day, Virginia watched Lisa: the way the camera followed her, the way she commanded the attention of all of the men that she came into contact with. Virginia felt some sort of affection for Lisa, one she couldn't explain, as she watched her handle Mr. Carter like he was nothing to her yet important at the same time. The boldness that was in Lisa's voice when she told him how unimportant he was, the curl in her fingers as she stroked his back as he stood staring at her, she looking at him deeply. Lisa had fascinated him and made him hate her at the same time. But he didn't leave, couldn't leave her side.

Virginia told her mother that she couldn't turn away—from the boldness of Lisa—as she was being whipped with a switch for cutting school. Ruby stopped mid-swing, looked at Virginia and saw something in her eyes that she hadn't seen before. Saw how her eyes softened when she spoke the white woman's name. What Virginia said with her eyes was far more damaging than the words that came out of her mouth "I did it to see her, Mama, to see Lisa." I'll be damned, Ruby thought to herself. I clean on my hands and knees so that this heifer can eat every day, and her eyes don't bend like that for me. Not one bit. I don't eat sometimes so that this one can have more, so she won't be skin and bones. I played with her, made sure that each breath was there, loved her more because she was what I remembered most. Ruby ran her eyes up and down her daughter's body like she had to remind herself who Virginia was. Who exactly was she? Ruby let the switch drop to the floor, shaking her head. "You love that white woman more than me?"

Thinking about her mother now doesn't make Virginia as nervous as it did before. Now she just laughs and thinks that her mother was right—she did love that white woman more. But not for the reasons her mother believed. Virginia stepped away from the railing and walked back into the apartment. She cursed out loud because her mouth needed to chew, and the sides of her jaws were now sore. Virginia needed the motion and the freedom that came with breaking the candy down to its smallest size, to take her mind off of what she knew was final.

"Shit," Virginia said out loud. "This boy is going to make me snatch his ass." Virginia pulled her blond hair into a ponytail, smeared some Vaseline on her lips, and slipped into a pair of blue house shoes that sat at the front door like eager puppies. The purple sundress she wore didn't match the shoes, but she didn't have time to change; she was sure that Gabriel would let his disdain be known. And besides, LeRoi was the habit she was trying to kick. When Virginia walked out the door, she almost bumped into Old Man, who was coming out the store.

"Whoa, pretty thing. You about to knock me over." Old Man walked with a limp and a wooden cane with elaborate carvings. His dark blue short-sleeved shirt contrasted against his fair skin; his pants were wrinkled and cuffed. He had a head full of black hair with a fist of gray in the front.

"Have you seen LeRoi?"

"It's been a minute. You know how my nephew is. Cut out like a ghost."

Virginia's eyes darted from him to the street. "Well, if he comes back, tell him I'm waiting."

"Will do, pretty lady. But if I was you, I wouldn't sit around too long. Good day."

Virginia watched Old Man walk away, and even in his limp, she saw the same arrogance that was in LeRoi. The same arrogance that allowed him to sing his way back into her life, as if he hadn't been gone for long periods of time. The thing that curved his lips as he hovered above her, knowing that she would beg him to finish, to bring her to climax; it was the same arrogance that told her that it was his world, not hers. A world that wanted him and only him — a world that killed him, lynched him, cut off his balls and stuffed them into jars, pockets, onto shelves, in dresser drawers, in listless night dreams because they were afraid, always afraid that someone else would take them. A world that knew it could not exist or sustain itself without her but never let on to that fact simply because it had him...

It was the same arrogance that coated her skin like sweat when she stood in front of all of those faces, the white men who used their eyes to devour her body while biting their lips, the pink tips of their tongues darting in and out, fantasizing about licking her, tasting every part of her black body.

It was this arrogance that sat in her chest and forced her to recall the laugher when she told them that she studied Shakespeare. The "Aye, Shakespeare, really?" that came before the tidal wave of laughter, the message underneath reverberating in her ear with each step that she took. Walking out of those auditions, she played with her hair, combing her fingers through it, obsessively—trying to rake out the arrogance. Her thighs hot with it, her armpits jelly. For a year Virginia kept going back—although giving up on the stories, she tried out for anything—but nothing met her like their arrogance which was in their eyes, lips, the gaping space between their legs, their whole beings.

Virginia shook her head at Old Man as he walked away and figured that he was lying. He knew were LeRoi was; that's what they do for each other, she thought, lie and keep each other safe. She turned away from Old Man and looked at her hands and then down to the mismatched socks that she wore. Who keeps me safe? she thought. Who looks out for and protects me? I used to. I used to make sure that no one stuck their pinky in my heart to scrape it, mark it, lay claim to it. I used to take care of me, and when I saw him in Lady's, I let that all go. I used to protect myself...

It had been weeks since Virginia slept in her bed; the sheets were still ruffled from when they made love. The room was empty save for a bed that came from Goodwill; a worn nightstand with a Mason jar top full of cigarette butts was covered with tiny, circular burn marks. Across from the bed was a dresser that had all of its knobs missing. On the top of the dresser was the framed picture of Lisa Hughes from *As The World Turns*, and a faded Bible. When LeRoi did come back, he would lay his guitar against the side of the dresser—the light wood contrasting against the blackness of the case. He was habitual in his return from wherever he had been. He would stand outside of her window playing his guitar, the melodies like soft hands waking her from a sleep that she could never remember falling into. The notes would shake her, caress her, and she would sit up in the bed. He would sing her a gin-laced song that would be an apology for his missing face:

> *Let me in to love you, girl.*
> *Let me in*
> *Let my arms hold you, girl*
> *Give me one more chance*
> *Let me in to love you*
> *Give me one more chance!*

Sometimes she would stand at the window and scream at him to leave, to go back to where he had come from, refusing to let him in. Other times, she would miss him so much that she would forget that he had disappeared and let him in to love her like the music promised to do. That night, after she let the music love her, she laid her head on his chest.

"Why do you stay away so long?"

"Ain't no time limit on the music, V."

Virginia traced his nipple. "What about me?"

"What you mean, 'What about me?'"

Virginia moved her ear over his heart and drummed her fingers to the beat. He was tall and yellow with freckles that looked like the tips of flames. His hair, slicked down with Dick's Pomade, curled at the ends. "What type of music you playing that keep you away for so long?"

"Why all the questions, V? I ain't known you to put a leash on anyone." LeRoi stroked her leg, letting his fingers rest in the pocket behind her knee.

"Sometimes, dogs need a leash."

"This dog has to roam free, woman. This one has to hold its own leash, make its own way."

"I don't want you to leave me again."

"Leave you, huh?"

"I can't take you being here when you feel like it, Roi."

"I don't know what to tell you, girl. I have to go where the music is. If it's in St. Louie, I am there. In Chi-town, I'm there. Can't stop it."

"There is music here." Virginia reached over him to the nightstand, pulled a Newport from its pack, and lit it. She inhaled deeply, let the smoke rest in her mouth for a minute, and looked at him. "When I was a little girl, I used to stand around and listen to my mother and aunt talk about the stories like it was their lives that they were watching. Like somehow the people on that show had a key to a life that they wanted, but couldn't have." She inhaled again and looked at her hands. "You know, I listened to them, and then one day I cut school to see the woman who made them happy *and* mad. I watched it and her, and I didn't feel the same way they did. I didn't want what the people on the stories had. I wanted my own. I wanted to be able to get it on my own. They had nice clothes. Nice kids. Nice everything. I didn't want their nice stuff. I wanted my own. I wanted my own and I set out to do so and man, I got everything I wanted. I got everything because I controlled how people looked at me. Baby, I had white men eating out of my hands. But you? You I have to chase. I have to beg you to stay. I ain't never begged no man to stay with me."

"Then don't start now." LeRoi pulled away from her and sat up so that his back was on the headboard. "I can't deal with this right now, girl."

"You can't deal with it? I sit here waiting on you, and you tell me you can't deal. Do I look like I need this? Like I need to be waiting on some guitar man to lullaby me? You don't need this? Hell, I don't need you." As soon as she said this, Virginia felt him pull away, felt giant oak trees growing in front of her eyes—roots clutching dirt, the branches shielding her from him. "I didn't mean that. I just need you here, Roi. Chance needs you."

"I ain't his father, so he don't need me. He got what he need. He got you. I need to make my music. I am something when I make my music. So if you think that you gon' stop me from making my music, then you smoking something stronger than them Newports." LeRoi jumped out of the bed and reached for his clothes.

If Virginia hadn't known better, she would have sworn that the tips of the flames danced on his face. The sun poked through the gray sky, and as he put on his pants one leg at a time, the roots dug deeper, the branches grew longer.

Virginia reached over, put the cigarette out on the top of the nightstand, and then got out of the bed. "Look, baby, you don't have to leave." She reached her arms out to him, and he zipped up his pants, stopped, and looked at her. He studied her and saw the difference. She was different from when they met in 1977. Then, she was hungry but not for him. She had a hunger for life like he did. He hungered for the quiet that the music gave him. She was hungry for what the world kept telling her that she couldn't have. He could be with her and not be tied down, and she was okay with that.

Back then, he had to work a little harder for her affection because she wasn't hungry for it, for him. Now she looked at him like she wanted to eat every bit of him from skin to bone to marrow, and he couldn't have her swallow him whole like they did in St. Louis in Memphis in Chicago while he played his guitar. LeRoi was young then, much too young to realize that hunger was deadly. That it forced men to do things that they would never do if they had been fed. He knew that look and how its teeth felt on his bones, and he couldn't let it happen this time. He was smarter this time. He knew better than to let the hunger eat away at him.

"So, you trying to eat me, too? You trying to take what's left of me, too?" LeRoi's voice trailed off, and then he looked back at her. The face was different, the lips protruded as if the teeth had grown, expanded; the eyes set back in their sockets as if determined and ready for war... "I'm gone, Virginia. I'm gone." He grabbed his white shirt and slipped it onto his arms. He worked in silence.

Virginia stood still as he finished buttoning up his shirt. Did he know that he was the reason that she got out of bed in the mornings, so that she could hurry the day away to go back to sleep so she could do it all over again? Wait for him to come back. Wait for him to put her back together because when he left, when he left, he took pieces of her with him. Pieces she didn't know existed until his absence made them noticeable, real. He couldn't have known, because if he did, if he did, then he would sit still and quiet the noise in his head. But he wasn't coming back this time, and she felt it as each button was pushed through the tiny slit made just for it. Each time his long fingers slid a button through its hole, it locked away more of him, secured him right out of her life. Virginia wanted to tell him he could leave whenever he wanted, that he could roam this earth as long as it took for him to play his music—as long as he came back to her and loved her with the music. Instead of saying that, she said what was wrapped in the pain that exploded in her chest the moment the last button slipped in its hole: "Ain't nobody trying to hear what you playing, anyway!"

Virginia watched the trees grow taller; the branches

grew and blossomed, the trees roots grew deeper as his hand rested on the knob of the door. He looked back at her one last time; she sat back on the bed and laid her head on the backboard. She played with the half-burnt cigarette in her hand. When he was gone and after the click of the lock meeting its resting place replayed over again in her head, she remembered what Rachel E. had asked her right before she was to meet the first white man she would let enter her: "How dangerous is an open heart?" Virginia didn't know then and couldn't answer. She shrugged her shoulders, and Rachel E. grabbed her with both of her hands and told her, "Very. An open heart is dangerous because it makes you forget what's at stake. What can be gained then lost by just a simple mistake." A simple mistake was what Virginia made when she loved LeRoi and let her heart open to him and let him dwell there when he had no intention of protecting it, had no idea of how the blood flowed for and to him.

Now she stood outside of the door and watched Gabriel flutter around the store. He moved like he always did, as if he owned everything and everyone around him. Her stomach curled, and her heart seemed to stutter-step, beating hard against her chest. This can't be, Virginia thought to herself. This can't be all that this life is. Can't be just hard candy to take the place of a man who can't sit still long enough to love me the way that I love him. Virginia walked in without looking at Gabriel and stood in front of the closet rack that held an assortment of Little Debbie snack cakes. She picked up an oatmeal cream pie. "Did Chance get my Lemonheads?"

"He did."

"Oh." Virginia fingered the small snack cake, and then put it back down. She walked to an aisle pretending to search for something. She felt Gabriel's eyes on her skin.

"It don't hurt to say hello, V. And he ain't back there!" Gabriel's voice followed her and settled over her like dust.

Virginia's hand rested on a box of Ritz crackers. She tried to think of something witty to say, something to show Gabriel that she was okay, that she could take care of herself, handle all of the things that he thinks that she can't. "Where is he?"

"I don't know, child. He flew in here, and flew right back out."

Virginia traced the outline of the slim box, letting her hand rest on the curve of the "R," then let her hands fall to her side. She didn't know what else to do with them, so she walked to the counter and rested her palms on the glass, staring at the candies that lined the shelves. "Did you give him my Newports?"

"You know I did. I had to sneak them because you know she's always watching me." Gabriel laughed and waited for Virginia to look at him.

"Thank you."

"You scared to look at me now, V? After all we been through, after all that I have done for you and your child, you have to talk to me with your head down?" Gabriel leaned in closer to Virginia's head, forcing her to look up.

"I just came for my candy and cigarettes. Nothing else."

"I wish you stop sending him down here to get them anyway."

"Mind your business, Gabriel."

"Look, I wouldn't have to mind *your* business if you did."

"Is this what you been waiting on, waiting on me so that you could show your ass?"

The smile on Gabriel's face slipped, and he gripped the edges of the counter. "I'm just trying to help."

"Your help always come with a price."

"Living in this world is a price, child. You just have to decide how much you willing to pay."

"Leave it alone, Gabriel."

Gabriel studied Virginia. She looked worse these days. The hair was always a mess—too light for her skin complexion and too stringy. Her skin was sallow; before, it was like wet velvet—smooth to the touch. Earlier, he had seen her outside, staring. He was tempted to open the door for her, to ask her if she needed him, but thought better of it. Nowadays, their conversations always ended up in a fight, ending nastier each time. He wished that the old Virginia would come back and reclaim her place in this world. "Have you looked in the mirror lately?"

Virginia tugged at the hair already falling out of the ponytail. "I don't have time for this."

"Apparently you don't have time for much. A hot oil treatment will do wonders for that kitchen of yours."

"Fuck you, Gabriel."

"That's what got you into trouble the first time." Gabriel's voice was flat, hard.

That familiar feeling rose up in Virginia again. The coating that she had finally managed to wash off began to fall and fold itself over her again. Even in a dress, Gabriel still had the same timbre in his voice, the same pride, afforded by virtue of his maleness. He could sit and tell her what to do with her legs, even though he had done nothing with his. And as much as Gabriel hated LeRoi, and as much as he talked to her about the uselessness of a man and the way that they corrupt you with their need to control, he is just like LeRoi and he thinks that he is not because he is in a dress. A black man in a dress. She tried to wipe the film from her face. When she moved her hands, she met Gabriel's smile and his batting eyelids. "Go to hell. Tell Chance to bring his ass home."

I remember the first time that I let a white man enter me. I didn't get paid like Rachel E. said I was supposed to. I was scared, too scared to take the money that he held out to me. His fingers were scarred and fat, scary like that hard ribbon candy you shouldn't eat because you know that it has been sitting for years. The money scared me more, I think, because it reminded me of the stuff that kidnappers hold out to the would-be kidnapped. I looked at the fat ribbon candy fingers, and I tried hard not to vomit. I held the bile in my throat while he was on top. His voice reminded me of a violin: lean, relentless. I tried to drown him out, his violin voice and the squeaking bed.

I thought about my hair. Rachel E. told me it needed to be lighter, straighter. I cried when I first saw it. Cried because I didn't know myself—I no longer saw the little girl who was plain and ordinary. For a brief moment, I missed that girl. I missed the cold and clammy hands of my brother and sisters, missed the lumps of oatmeal that stuck in my throat as I tried to swallow, missed the thumping of the double dutch ropes against the ground, the rhythms steady like a heartbeat. I missed my mother. But it didn't help, this hair, at least not at the auditions. I didn't get parts, and I was hungry, and the hotel where I had made a declaration that I was going to be famous was about to throw me out.

That first night, I stood there. In front of him. My arms wrapped around myself. He patted the bed, his ribbon-candy fingers made an indent in the worn spread. Little specks of dust shot up from the space that he patted. I couldn't move at first, and I tried to remember what Desdemona felt like when she was in love with Othello. What did she feel when he strangled her with his love and not his hands? Passion, my teacher Mrs. Day said, was what Othello had. I believed that he wanted to kill what he saw in himself through her eyes: hopelessness. I finally sat next to him, and he took his hands and knuckled my breasts with his eyes closed. His lips parted, and I turned my head, afraid that he wanted a kiss. He didn't even wait for me to take off my blue sundress or my white high-heeled sandals that I borrowed from Rachel E. It took me two hours to pick out that dress, out of her closet, and he didn't pay it any attention. His weight took the air out of my body; his teeth scraped my nipples, and, with the pain, they got hard.

Before that night, I moved in with Rachel E. and she

taught me how to get men, said that we weren't prostitutes, just women who really liked the company of men who had money. Her cream-colored fingers applied my makeup while I sat with rocks in my stomach. "Now," she said, "you look like you are worth something." He was big, this white man, with hair on his chest that looked like he had a bear lapping at his chin. He stroked my cheekbone, said that I had pretty, chocolate candy-bar skin. Nothing about my hair. Nothing, and while his violin voice and squeaking bed melded into one beat, I thought about my mother and what she would say if she saw me here on my back. What would she think now? I closed my eyes, and when I opened them, she was standing over him, switch in hand, arm raised mid-air, ready to beat me like she did the day I told her I wanted to be like a white woman on TV. I let out a small noise, and he looked at me. "Is it good to you?" I didn't answer. I closed my eyes and wished my mother away.

3

That morning, after dreaming of a sweet girl named Eunice, Old Man heard the front door slam. It was his nephew LeRoi, and it had taken Old Man a while—six years in fact—to get used to the boy being here. LeRoi was thirty-eight, but to Old Man, who was almost seventy, he was still a boy. A boy who was a fool with a taste for no-use jazz (a guitar at that!), women who held on too tight, and bars that served hard liquor.

Old Man sat up in the bed and looked out the window. The sun was just beginning to rise and he could feel its rays gently massaging his good leg. The bad leg, the one that required him to lean-walk, was under the covers. He treated the bad leg with indifference—it had been mangled and shriveled like redwood bark for over thirty years and he kept it covered at all times unloved.

LeRoi's running up then back down the stairs agitated Old Man. He had told that boy a million times that he had to be gentle with stairs, not abuse them with the bottoms of his feet. LeRoi hadn't learned that lesson yet, and Old Man knew that treating things (other than his guitar) with kindness was not something his nephew did very often.

It pained Old Man to see Virginia lose her mind over him, and when he saw her standing outside of Lee's the other day, he felt awful telling her that LeRoi was gone. But he knew that it wasn't his place, or his business. Still, the way LeRoi treated Virginia would have killed his mother, Eunice, for sure if she knew of it. One thing Old Man believed about his nephew was that there wasn't anything good left in him but his strumming fingers.

Old Man spoke out loud to his legs, "It's time to make it." He stood on the hardwood floor, and then limped to a high-backed chair that his cane leaned on. He found the cane in the Goodwill on Selma Boulevard. It was dark oakwood with faces carved in it. He was drawn to it the moment he saw it, and when he picked it up and ran his hands across the eyes, raised cheekbones, short, sharp noses, he cried. Soft tears at first, and when they became loud sobs, the store clerk ran to him, "Sir, are you okay?" Old Man wiped the tears from his face with the backs of his hands and looked up to the store clerk. "I'm fine, young lady, I'm fine. But I will take this. Yes. I will take this." Now he leaned all of his weight on the cane and lean-walked out of the room down the stairs.

LeRoi was sitting in the front room.

"Are you running from the Devil or something?" Old Man stood in the entrance to the front room, looking at his nephew holding his guitar. The room, sparsely furnished, had a green couch with red shams. In the middle of the room was a black card table with three fold out chairs; the other one, LeRoi sat in. The walls were bare. Curtains as thin as baby's hair hung from the window.

"Not running from nothing."

"Could have fooled me the way you cut out from upstairs." He looked at his nephew's side view and saw Eunice's chin and long, wide nose. "What you doing home so early? It's not like you to be up before the sun."

"Had things to do."

"Like what? You haven't had things to do in a long time."

LeRoi looked at his uncle and ran his fingers along the base of his guitar. "Her strings needed to be tightened. I got a gig coming up."

"Oh, really?" Old Man lean-walked into the room and sat on the couch. He reached down and lifted the crushed redwood to the table. "When this happen?"

"Juney called me last week and said they need someone to fill out the band. Add something to the sound. So I told him I would."

"Huh? Haven't heard you talk about Juney in a long time. Didn't know he was still playing a band. Huh."

"That's all you got to say is 'Huh'? I'm going to be playing again."

"You *been* playing son. At least that's what you tell me, so what's different this time?"

"You sound like Virginia."

"Well, I guess we both make sense then." Old Man leaned up and looked LeRoi over. There was dusk in his eyes, and he was disheveled; his hands looked like crumpled sandpaper. "When you gon' sit still?"

"What do you all want from me?"

"I take it the 'you all' means me and Virginia."

LeRoi tightened a string and then cut his eyes at his uncle. "She has been riding my back ever since I told her I was going back out on the road. I thought she would be happy."

"Well," Old Man said, "did you talk to her before you told Juney you would go?"

"Why would I do that?"

"She is your woman, right?"

"Now you really sound like her." LeRoi laughed. "We don't talk anymore. We fuck, argue about me always leaving, and then fuck again."

"Seems to me something could be said in all that time, you know? Something while you lay up in her house."

"Well, like I said, we don't talk. We used to." LeRoi lowered his head and wondered if his uncle ever wanted something other than what he had.

"What about the boy?" Old Man tried to cross his good leg over the bad, thought about it more, and then stopped.

"What about him?"

"What about him? You 'bout the closest thing he got to a daddy."

"I'm not his daddy. And I didn't sign up for it, either."

"You signed up for it when you lay down with his mama."

"Like I told her, he ain't my responsibility. And he got that fag, Gabriel.

Old Man winced at the word "fag." He remembered

the first time he saw Gabriel's legs sticking out of that box, in the alley between Lee's and the Methodist church. Back then Old Man had a funny feeling about a man dressed like a woman. He had heard people talk about it, but had never seen it in person. He was ready to kill Gabriel when he saw him stand, all six feet of him, but Lee talked him down. Now he had an affinity for Gabriel that his nephew would not understand. "What does one have to do with the other?"

"No one understands," said LeRoi. "I wish Onion was still here. He knew what I was feeling before I knew, like I was a piece of skin attached to his body, you know. He knew me and could tell when I just needed to go. He knew when I got that feeling that I couldn't shake."

Old Man laid the walking stick across his lap and started humming. His eyes darted from his nephew to the card table to the lamp that sat on the end table. He knew how a whispering thing could drive someone to do things they're not fully aware of. He understood how it makes someone believe that it is the one and only best thing. Old Man knew this, and he hummed louder, a bluesy tune, trying to beat back that whispering thing that had haunted him for years. Tormented him from the time he laid eyes on her thirteen-year-old skin, the blackness a sharp contrast to his redness. The eyes, wide like an expectant mother, calling him even though they were too young to know that they were; *instinct* is what he told her when he was finally inside her. It was a natural instinct to run to the one you love. She was his niece. Eunice. The first time Old Man entered her, he felt a completeness that no years of searching could do. While he caressed her young thigh, all the walking became worth it, all the miles that hardened the balls of his feet, worth it.

Afterward, Eunice leaned into him, breathing heavy in his ear, tickling his eardrum so that he laughed, even in the heat of seriousness—suddenly making him aware of his age and her innocence. She said, "I will wait." Wait? Huh. Wait on me. On me. Old Man knew that the wait would kill him, and his sister, too, if she found out, so he slid out of town, rode far away from St. Louis. But it wasn't enough. That whispering thing still followed him. Made him look over his shoulder. Made him question whether or not he was losing his mind. The back of his ear still burned with the heat of her lips, and every time he lay still, he felt her young body pressing against his. The lips like death, always looming but waiting its turn.

What could he do? Old Man used to think to himself when he was sitting on his sister's porch in St. Louis, watching Eunice jump rope—a thing that he knew she was too old for, but doing it anyway, he thought, or would have bet his life on, just for him. The turning of the rope like his mind: turning over and over again the possibility of waiting. A whispering thing.

"That thing," Old Man pointed to LeRoi's guitar, "will pull you in all directions if you let it." Old Man shrugged his shoulders, then stroked the gray hairs on his chin. "Anyway, nowadays ain't nothing being said with those instruments. I bet you all don't even know how to use them right. Don't know how to make them cry and moan like they supposed to. I bet." Old Man nodded his head up and down.

LeRoi got up from the chair and held his guitar close to his chest. He walked around the room, bobbing his head back and forth to a beat only he could hear. "This is it for me. This is the last thing I got. The only thing, and ain't nothing no one can tell me about it. I am it, and we are the same. You dig, Uncle? So stop jiving me like you made some music with your life. I tell my story with this." LeRoi lifted the guitar as evidence.

"Tell a story? Boy, you too young to have much of a story. It ain't nothing but bits and pieces."

"Bits and pieces? Huh. Bits and pieces? I been in bits and pieces since I left St. Louie." LeRoi stroked absently at his guitar. "Hell, someone, anybody, pick me up along the way 'cause I can't figure it out. I can't figure out what I mean. I'm in someone else's pocket, stuck to the bottom of someone else's shoe. All over the place, Unc. I got a story. It's just all over the place." He looked at his uncle and tried to picture him young and splattered all over the place. All in tiny pieces. A shudder went down his spine.

"I still think you wasting your time with that thing."

"Without it, my life would be a waste." LeRoi looked past his uncle, gripping his guitar closer to his chest. His fingers plucked lightly against the strings. How did black men do it? LeRoi thought as he focused his eyes on the strings of the guitar. How did they stay sane when they saw themselves being plucked apart, picked like leftover meat on a stew bone, littered, and scattered all over the place? How did black men do it? How did they work things out in the head when all of it isn't there? When the mind is on missing fathers, on nightmares worn like heavy coats? How did black men do it? How did they walk these streets day in and day out, hunting, scavenging, looking for themselves—when their legs were constantly being torn from under them, their feet, toes, heels, arches shredded...

How did black men cope when, as little boys, they stood and watched their mothers blow off their fathers' smiling, pleading faces? The skin flying like pieces of candy knocked out of hanging piñatas? How did they deal with nightmares that crouched like shadows and snuck up on them as they replayed the smiling, pleading faces of their fathers scattered over the beige carpet that their mothers had spent all afternoon cleaning? How did they do it? How did they bounce back from that? Bounce back enough to play catch with their sons whose looks bypassed theirs but snuck back in time to steal the smiling, pleading faces? The ones that they could never get out of their minds; the faces that made them pack up one day because the memory was too much—the scattering reminding them of their vulnerability? How did they constantly do it when they knew their lives were in danger, that the very thing that they were would kill them? That the very thing that they hunted at night was only a mirror away, a quick glance in clear, gray glass?

And if they looked, then what? Would they be able to finally gather all the falling, scattered pieces and put them back together again? Capture and hold on to the only face—smiling and pleading—that made sense to them? Make life bearable? At last, maybe, something to help them look at the faces that they abandoned because they were afraid of the spaces in the brown, yellow, red, charcoal skin. The spaces that exposed—spaces that let the world in to destroy. LeRoi didn't know how they did it, and if they could tell him, if his uncle could tell him how he has made it this far without having all of him, then maybe, maybe, he could figure himself out.

Some days, Old Man missed the peace and quiet that living alone brought. But he loved Eunice more than peace, and even though she was long gone—and nowhere to be found—he would do anything for her. Still sitting in the same place, Old Man stroked his bad leg. He felt a dull ache every time he touched it, and he thought about Eunice. She told him to wait. Told him that she would come back to St. Louis, come back for him. He waited. When three years had passed, and he was numb, he had walked to the post office on 16th Street and Market. He had promised his mother a letter at least once a month, and no matter where he was, he tried very hard to keep that promise.

It was a cold Monday in September 1955, and after mailing the letter, he walked out the front door and saw a woman with skin as dark as a bruised plum and calves he knew tasted just like Eunice's. Old Man stopped, looked harder and knew that he could spot her in any crowd, in any packed room, smoky concert hall. He started towards her, reached out his hand to her and started jogging. He followed her as she walked past City Hall and then the Justice Center; he watched her as the plum legs cut over to Spruce. He moved so fast that he didn't have breath to call out to her, so he kept his hand outstretched and hoped that she could feel him. She moved faster, as if she knew he was following her, and he tried to keep up. It has to be her. Ain't no way that it's not her. I waited like she said. Made myself sit still for three years, three years. Kept the cold from eating away at me, the restlessness from stuffing itself down my throat, from suffocating me... I got to touch her. If I feel her skin I will know it's her, and she will know it's me. Know that I waited like she said. Hid all parts of myself from other women. Wouldn't let them in, wouldn't let them see me. I need to feel it, need to see. Need to ask her why she stayed away so long, why she made me wait so long. Didn't she know that I would? Didn't she know that all I remember is the way her breath felt on my ears, hot like the Tennessee sun I ran from. Maybe she didn't know. Maybe she wanted to see if I would, if I would prove myself to her. She wanted me to work harder for her. If I can just touch her skin, maybe it will tell me that she really meant to come back, that she didn't mean to make me wait so long. Maybe, maybe. If only she would slow down, the legs, the legs, I can taste them, the legs, I waited. I...

Finally, he called out her name: "Eunice," and when the woman turned around, Old Man saw that she was not Eunice, his face twisted, and he looked away to hide the shame, fear, lust, panic, so that he didn't see the hole in the street. In the hospital, the doctors told him that he had mangled his leg, and as the nurse wrapped his leg, he whispered her name—"*Eunice.*"

A small-framed nurse with big hands woke Old Man as she checked his bandages. He looked up at her brown, smiling face, and he could tell by the way that she touched him that she was a mother. She was patient. Her nametag read Holloway.

"This is going to hurt a little bit. But I will do my best." She took out a pair of scissors and started to cut the blood soaked bandages. Old Man tried not to look, but he couldn't stop himself, and when he looked down he saw the leg that looked like the roots of trees.

He winced.

"It's not that bad. We will get it back to normal." She deftly pulled the cut bandages off, and Old Man didn't feel the skin that clung to the bandages. "You must have had a real bad accident."

"I wasn't paying attention to where I was going."

"What was that important that you would hurt yourself this bad?" Old Man didn't feel the saline solution that she squirted on the leg but jumped when she applied the iodine to the wound. "I'm sorry, sir. Have to do this. It will help it heal faster." Nurse Holloway smiled and winked at Old Man as she prepared to wrap the leg. "Maybe this is a blessing in disguise. Maybe you will sit still for a while."

Old Man watched the big hands of the nurse as she applied the bandages. The longest he had sat still was right before he left Memphis. He was fourteen when he left, but Old Man was restless long before that. Restlessness turned into hunger. A hunger that made him leave in 1927. His mother, Pearl, was a Cherokee Indian, and his father, Walter Johnson, was a sharecropper. They lived in a three-bedroom house on Old Allen Road, and he was the oldest of three. His sister, Trish, married Joseph and had three kids; his brother, Haskel, married June and had four children; Eunice, his niece, was his sister's youngest child.

Old Man was twelve when he started walking. He got up one day, sat on the porch of his house, looked into the sky, and wondered what else was out there. What else was there besides watching his father break his back and not profit from it, and his mother sitting and watching it happen? He wanted to know what else there was, other than what he was learning in his class books and what he saw his family going through. Somehow, he thought, things (more interesting) were happening around him, were different in other places. And since he saw what Memphis was doing to his father (making him almost unbearable, surly) and to his mother (always singing cryptic hymns)—he knew that sitting around dreaming of possibilities wouldn't sustain him.

One afternoon, while he sat behind his desk at Manassas Junior High School, he saw the map of the world stretched out on a wooden table in the back. He got up, walked to it, traced the shapes of the different cities in the United States with his fingers and walked back and forth in the classroom. His teacher, Ms. Burke, with bangs that almost covered her eyes and light dusky skin, stopped the reading lesson and said, "Odell Johnson, why are you pacing in my classroom?" He looked at her and replied, "I'm testing my path."

On the way home from school, Odell walked right past Old Allen Road, up to the top of the hill and right to the middle of town. By the time he got home, his father was waiting on him with a switch, and then Old Man decided that there was nothing left for him and that it was time to go. Odell snuck away in the safety of darkness; his mother—accustomed to her children's sleeping patterns— held her own breath until he had made it down the rickety stairs, and then sang a hymn that followed with each step that he took.

Odell's feet took him to Alabama, where he eventually found work in a pig slaughterhouse and where he lived with a woman named Bessie who let him sleep in her pantry for a few chores around her house. His red skin glistened in the yellow sun despite the cold air; his hair was black all over except for a spot of gray the size of a fist. While he cut the entrails out of recently silenced pigs, the still-screaming ones played in his head like a scratched Okeh record. The warehouse in which he did his mercy killing was the only one that let niggers walk in with the white folks. Once inside, all of them did the same thing: killed to survive. Killed to feed and keep their families afloat. The dirt floors were slippery with blood, and the steam from the boiling pots cooked the blood that dripped from the pink bodies that hung from meat hooks. The air of the factory had a stench that people could smell a mile away. When a pig was dipped in the scalding water, everyone stopped what they were doing, looked at each other, and shook their heads slightly. The niggers stopped because they saw their own bodies, heads cracked open, bodies split down the middle, being dipped; the white folks stopped because they saw themselves doing the cracking and dipping.

Odell's work at the slaughterhouse—cleaning out the

insides of the belly and sleeping with Bessie every once in a while—kept him still. When the shifts were over and the white folks went back to being white folks, the men that worked beside Odell—old, young, tired black men—would make fun of him about the fist of gray in his head. They sat around, their hands stained a deep purple with the blood of pigs, their boots and the bottoms of their pants legs soiled with pig shit. They passed around tobacco rolled in newspapers and made fun of each other.

"You ain't nuttin' but a pup. What you doing with that gray hair?"

"He been runnin' from the law all his natural life. They scared him shitless," said a man in his sixties—his back curved first from years of picking cotton, now from stooping to pick up pig balls.

"Hell, I bet he got an old lady drivin' him crazy. You ain't no goddam pup. You an Old Man."

They all broke into a nervous laughter because if the young were getting old faster, then the life they thought they had lived was nothing at all.

The elderly man with the curved back looked at Old Man and waved him over. His hand, which held the cigarette, was cracked and stained with pigs' blood. "What you gon' do with yo' life, boy?"

Old Man reached his hand out for the burning-too-fast cigarette. He put it in his mouth and inhaled it slowly. "I don't know. I know I won't be here much longer."

"You just got here. Plant yo' feet for a change."

"My feet the ones keep me moving."

Old Man left Alabama a month later and ended up in

Kentucky shining shoes at a bus depot. When he looked up one day from a pair of black patent leather shoes on a white man in a Palm Beach suit made of gabardine, he packed up his cans of Nugget shoe polish, his brushes, and moved again.

His sister Trish moved her family to St. Louis, and Old Man figured that it would be just a resting spot until he could find another place suitable. When Old Man saw Eunice, something happened to him. There was now a space, an opening, where there wasn't one before. It was small at first, something that he felt slightly. And he tried hard, at first, to ignore the opening, the thing that was happing inside of him. Since he had been a teenager, no woman had moved him. No woman had kept his interest past the moist hole used to please him. He used to watch people dote over their children, husbands loving their wives, and he could tell that they were somehow satisfied. Somehow fulfilled in a way that he would never be. When he really saw her: her thirteen-year-old self, long black pigtails, Vaselined black skin, and dainty lemon knee socks, not the little girl whose diapers he had changed or bounced on his knee, he felt for the first time that he could be satisfied. Sitting on the porch watching her jump, his eyes following the rope, the small thing, opened up more.

Old Man knew what he was doing when he pulled her into the pantry. Her dress was crisscrossed in the back and as yellow as the sun. Her black skin felt like velvet on his palms. He kissed her, slowly at first, and when she parted her lips to let him in, he became more forceful. What if she changed her mind? he thought. What if she realizes that he is too old for her? Old Man ran his fingers up and down her smooth black arms and felt himself blinded by the sun that swallowed her. He heard himself panting heavily and was suddenly embarrassed. He backed away from her, but she pulled him back, taking his hands and placing them on her tiny waist. He pulled her closer, and then laid her down like one would a little baby doll. She wrapped her arms around his neck. When he entered her tight flesh, he let out a small scream, and he couldn't tell who was crying harder, her or him.

4

This was always the hard part: coming back, defeated. Leaving was easy because there was always promise in the adventure, some hope of solace in the music. The music calmed LeRoi, made those tiny pricks of pain bearable, but this time it was different. In Cincinnati, LeRoi's hands wouldn't slow down enough for him to play his guitar. As he tried to stroke the strings, catch up with the melody, he saw all the women who wanted to eat his hands. It wasn't new, these visions, but he had learned, somehow, to keep them at bay. But the night he and Virginia argued, he saw her slide each of his fingers into her mouth, and it came back then, that feeling like in St. Louis, Detroit, New Orleans, Memphis, and Chicago. LeRoi walked off the stage and out the front door because his hands wouldn't stay still long enough for him to play. That was three nights ago and when he got back to Cleveland, he caught the Number 3 bus to 125th and Superior, got off, and walked down St. Clair into the Low Down, walked straight to the jukebox, and slid in a coin. He stood there for the rest of the night, sliding coins into the metal box with the hope that it would slow his hands down.

In St. Louis, it started when his mother didn't come home. Then, at twelve, that absence he thought was too large, too impossible to handle. Later he realized that it was the beginning of the gnawing.

I was twelve then. Woke up, you know, looking for her. She was all that I had then. And all that I thought I needed. She worked at Alice's on Chester. And I had to stay home alone because we didn't have anyone to watch me. I was twelve, you know. She said that I was her little man and that I would be okay until she got home. At first I couldn't go to sleep; I would sit up all night waiting on her, and when I heard her heels clicking on the wood floor, I would fall asleep. In the mornings, I would stare at her and ask her why she had to work at night, and she would stroke my cheek. She never said a word. Then she would do it all over again. Every night, and then one day I was able to sleep, able to sleep with her not being there. I wonder sometimes if that is the reason why she didn't come home that night. Did she think that I was okay, that since I could sleep without hearing her heels click against the wood floor, I didn't need her? I am a grown man now, and the sound of high heels stops me dead in my tracks.

I was twelve and before she left that night, she sat at the kitchen table longer, kept sipping on that white teacup even though it was empty. She sat at the table and then jumped up and rushed out. She worked at Alice's Juke Joint, and when I woke up, she wasn't there. I got out of bed and sat at the kitchen table, and when she didn't come through the door, I pissed myself. I was twelve and pissed myself because my mother didn't come through the door. Shit, I sat in my piss for a good hour, and when I started to shiver, I got up and changed. I changed but left the piss in the kitchen chair because if she came back, she would see that I pissed myself 'cause I was scared that she wasn't coming back.

I walked to Alice's to find her. To see if she was just working late or something. Walking there something was eating at me, you know, gnawing at me, but I didn't know what it was. Couldn't know really—I was twelve. I was twelve and didn't know if my mama would find my piss and be worried or mad. Didn't know if she would shake her head in disgust or in shame for making her little man worry that much. I walked into Alice's and stood against the wall. Stood there hoping that I would hear her clicking against the floor.

LeRoi scanned the room. No one was in the Low Down that he recognized. His partnas, Ship and CJ, were usually regulars, spending the money they earned from the barbershop before their old ladies got hold to it. Friends who didn't get him but knew enough not to ask too much about him, or from him. He put another coin into the box, and the guitar riff from "Purple Haze" startled him.

She wasn't there, but the sweetest sounds I had ever heard were. I didn't know where it came from but I walked closer. It was dark, but not too dark that I couldn't see the stage. They were on it. Black men palming instruments. I stood there.

"Aw, come on Douchey, what you waiting on? You gon' play that horn or what?"

"As soon as you hit dem drums, my man."

"You can't play them drums, fool. You got clubs for fingers."

"Ha! You tell 'em Sammy!"

"Aw, shut up, Lou, 'cause that nigger can't scat to save his life."

"Douchey, those lips of yours so big, they can't even fit around her head!"

I watched them tease each other, and then they started playing, and I forgot why I was there. I forgot that I had pissed myself and that I came to look and not listen to men play. I fell into the gaps, into the shell of the beats. They bounced off of each other; the music was alive, and when the horns rang out, the drums picked them up, carried them to the piano. And the piano gathered everybody and took them home. Filled the spaces that the others had created. I had never heard anything like it and haven't since. I play all the time partly to get that night back. That music that grew and expanded, then conflated right in front of me. I thought there was nothing else that mattered then. Nothing else that could top that. And then he walked on stage.

He was tall and black and carried a guitar and something that looked like a speaker. He then plugged the guitar into the speaker and played a note that made my groin tingle. I felt like I needed to relieve myself. I no longer felt that sense of fear or dread that I felt walking to Alice's. I let the chords take me. And with each note he played, my mother's face faded away. The emptiness was filled. I remember moving closer to the stage, closer to the guitar, swaying, moving my head to the complications in the music. When I opened my eyes, everyone was staring at me.

"Boy, what you doing here at this time of morning?" the one with clubs for hands said.

"I'm looking for my mama."

"Who yo' mama?" the one whose lips couldn't fit said as he wiped down his horn with a red oilcloth.

"Eunice." I didn't look at them but at the tall black man with slicke- back black hair. He was dressed in a pair of black slacks, wingtipped black shoes, and a white shirt that seemed to glitter, even in the darkness. He had a cigarette in one hand and a guitar in the other.

"She ain't here. Left a long time ago and I suspect she be looking for you, so you best get going."

"Let the young blood stay for a minute." the tall black man said.

"I'm out of here."

"Me too. You deal with it."

The men walked away, and the tall black man came from the stage.

"What's yo' name, young blood."

"LeRoi."

"What you doing here, young blood? You like what you see?"

I stared hard at the guitar that the man held like one would a newborn baby.

"Aww. You like this? " The man held the guitar out. "You ever touch one? Hold one? Play one? "

"No sir, " I said.

"I ain't old enough to be nobody's sir. They call me Onion 'cause I make all the women cry when I play Sally."

"Why you call it Sally?"

"'Cause you got to love her like a woman, and you can't love a woman with no name, can you? Naw, young blood, you can't love a nameless woman, and this here is the only woman I'm gon' *ever have."*

I was confused and reached for the guitar. Onion snatched it back and held it close to his chest.

"Have you ever held a woman?"

"No."

"Then you ain't ready to hold this one." Onion lowered the guitar and pulled a case from behind the stage. He placed it in the case, snapped it closed and looked at me. "Boy, before you can play her, you have to love her, and in order to love her, you have to have her. You get what I'm saying?"

"No."

Onion shook his head at me and smiled. A few years later, he told me that I reminded him of his little brother, and that that night, right then and there, he decided that I would become his little brother and that he would look out for me. "I tell you what, if you get yo' mama to let you hang out with me, I will teach you about Sally... But you got to ask yo' mama and you got to listen to these people before you come back to me. How is yo' memory?"

"Good, Onion. I can name all the Presidents and everything."

"That's good, boy, but that ain't what I'm interested in. Can you remember lists?"

"Yeah, I remember the grocery list all the time."

"Remember these names: Charlie Christianson, Monk, Bird, Parker, and Armstrong. Get them and listen to them. Listen to how they tell a story with their instruments. Let them talk to you, boy, and I guarantee you they will teach you a few things about loving a woman."

The song ended, but the melody stayed with him; the music trembled in his blood. The heart muscle scared him because it forced him to think about it. Think about it even after all of these years. It stank, really—clogged up his head and when he played, Lord, when he played, it created space.

Onion saved me that night. I didn't tell him that my mama never came back, and if he knew, he never said. I sat in that club and other clubs watching and mimicking the thick fingers stroking the razor-sharp strings. When I was with Onion and learning to play the guitar, I didn't think. I didn't feel. I didn't want her. When it was quiet and no music played, I made up tunes in my head, hummed them to myself to help. I mastered the guitar, you know, and one day I left Onion. I left and made my way through St. Louis, Chicago, Memphis, New Orleans, New York, and Detroit. Playing. Hiding. Playing until I was exhausted; playing until I was so tired that thinking about her wasn't an option. I played for her, really. Hoping that she would one day be there, sitting, at the back in the dark, smoke circling her head, watching and hearing the pain, the thunder in my song, and know. And I would hear the clicking, and then I would take over the set, play her right out the door.

"Can I ask you a question?"

LeRoi looked up, and Portia was standing in front of him. "What?"

She handed him a drink. "Crown and Coke, right?"

"You know that already, Portia. What do you want?"

"Why do you keep coming back?"

"Why do you care?"

"Because you always end up in my bed and then leave

me high and dry."

LeRoi took a long swallow of the drink and swirled the ice with the tip of his finger. His eyes rested on her breasts, the magical breasts, and he smiled. "I have no intention of being in your bed tonight."

"Oh, yeah?"

"Yeah."

"So, I guess she letting you back in, huh?"

LeRoi drank the rest of the drink and handed the glass to Portia.

Portia held the glass and scanned his face. There was never desire in it when he looked at her. Never anything that indicated that he wanted her past the time he was in her bed. Portia knew that it was indifference. Indifference hurt worse than cruelty, and Portia knew that he really cared about Virginia, even if he didn't say it. "You don't come back for me…"

She tried to eat my hands one night. I played in Chicago, and she sat at the table closet to the stage. Lanky and glossy like milk chocolate, she moved her leg to the music, her red shoe hanging off her toe, her calves losing themselves in the melody. She didn't smile, but I felt her eyeing me, the arch of her heel calling to me. When the set was over, she stood next to me and whispered in my ear. After we made love, she told me that my music had moved her, made her want to leave her skin. She played with my hands. Rubbed them gently, kissed the knuckles, and licked the tips of my fingers. I watched her put my fingers in her mouth and start to chew. I snatched my hand away. I got nervous, and she just smiled and licked her lips and then said, "What's wrong, baby?" I shuddered. That was the first time

anyone had tried to eat my fingers, and after that, I no longer
made love to women—I fucked them. Making love required my
hands; I could fuck without my hands, fuck without being tender
with my hands, and I did just that. Had to protect them, needed
them to play the music, keep the spaces going so that I could
retreat into them when I needed to.

"They told me about you."

"What they tell you about me?"

"That you no good, Roi. And that I should leave you alone."

"Then why didn't you listen?"

"I wish I had." Portia kissed his forehead and sighed heavily. "What you doing here, Roi? I thought you were done with you and me."

"I am." LeRoi kicked the covers off of his legs and crossed them Indian style. He looked at Portia. He fucked her last night; he was rough and didn't say a word. He had come back with a lot on his mind, and he knew that going to Virginia's or his uncle's wouldn't help. Portia didn't require much.

Portia ran her fingers across his thighs. "I don't mean nothing to you, do I?"

"I told you that you should have listened to them."

"I'm always fooling myself, Roi."

"I told you that this was just something to do." He reached for one of her magical breasts and cupped it.

Portia moved his hand away and watched it fall naturally to the space between his legs. "If I was her, you wouldn't just fuck me and leave. You wouldn't play with me like this."

"But you aren't her." LeRoi uncrossed his legs and leaned forward.

"Get out then... Go back to that bitch." Portia rolled to the other side of the bed and closed her eyes real tight.

The Low Down was no longer empty. LeRoi leaned back on the jukebox and watched people come and go— their faces like block glass, reflecting the room but not letting anyone see them on the inside. No real space to dance, but no one cared. Hips moved and stuck together in the middle of the room. Women were draped like lace doilies across the arms of the men. Men handled the complicated lace gently, as if they were in danger of tearing it, fingers firm but tender. The smoke that hovered on the floor earlier now rose to cover and hang off their bodies like capes. LeRoi had never danced before he met Virginia. Had never loved anyone other than his mother before her, had never tried hard to impress anyone. He was clumsy around her back then. Almost slicing his finger on guitar string, tripping over his feet. He walked past, and her eyes slid over him causally... She didn't lean into him or arch her back when he stood in front of her, like the other women did; he played with his hands, told her she was like music, like remembering. LeRoi thought of her when she left. Played that spot—Lady's Place of Jazz— every week until she came back. He stayed because he wanted to tell her that she was like the burn at the back of the throat after a long drag on a cigarette...like rainwater that glistens and hums after the storm, Virginia...like cool, ocean hush, Virginia...

Virginia didn't try and eat my hands. She loved them as much as I did. She got my music; I never had to explain it to her. When I played, her face had the same longing as my music; she felt me without knowing why. That's why I stayed that night— that's why I kept pulling my guitar out, strumming for her. For me. It was good, me and Virginia. Good, and I was content, not jumpy. Settled. Not as hungry as before. And when it came over me, that feeling, she let me leave, let me go play it away and didn't complain. Didn't follow me to the door, didn't kiss me goodbye. She watched and was there when I came back…

Then. Then, my hands got shaky, slow at first, but got worse when Virginia changed—or was it when Chance changed? He was always there then. Always around, looking, craving me, too. I asked her why she couldn't send him away. Why he couldn't be with the fag. She just looked then, her mouth slack, teeth partially showing. I watched them both then, watched them both watch me, and I stopped playing for her. She wanted to eat more than my hands; she wanted to eat all of me. All of me, and then I was out the door, out the door up the street, and I felt her watching, felt her teeth, saw the mouth widened, the teeth. She stood and watched me, my hands in my pockets, afraid to let them free.

They shook more then, more than they had before, and I couldn't stop thinking about her, couldn't stop thinking about the heels clicking on the floor, and each time I thought I heard the heels, they shook harder. I played harder, but nothing would make them stop; nothing could make the clicking heels fade. Nothing could erase the piss that followed me as I looked for her in St. Louis, Chicago, Memphis, Detroit, New York, New

Orleans… The music was leaving me, and I had to get it back. I had to stop Virginia from eating my hands. From eating all of me.

He stood outside of her building. His guitar was across his back, but he strummed an imaginary tune with his fingers. The windows to her apartment were dark. LeRoi opened the door and walked up the dank stairs. The last time he was here, she sat and watched him leave, her legs opened but closed to him. Now he wanted to talk her out of loving him so hard. Make her realize that that much love he couldn't handle, couldn't decipher. He wanted to come back but only if she didn't love so hard, so completely. He knocked on the door, lightly at first. After a minute, he banged harder.

"She ain't there." Gabriel stood in his open doorway.

"I didn't ask you."

"Hell, you didn't have to. But banging on the door ain't gon' make her appear, either."

LeRoi kept his back turned to Gabriel. His hatred of Gabriel was acute. LeRoi knew that he was putting shit in Virginia's head. He tried to keep her away from Gabriel, but when he was gone, Gabriel was there. And she told LeRoi that every time that he came back. "Who you think here when you gone, Roi?" It was bad enough that she wanted to strangle him with her love, but she tightened the rope every time she threw Gabriel in his face—made his absence and worthlessness greater with Gabriel's presence… "Where is she?"

"I don't think that she wants you looking for her."

"Look, punk!" LeRoi turned to face Gabriel. "I don't have time for this shit. Do you know where she is?"

"Ha! I tell you what. How about you roam up and down the streets like she does when you not around? Then you might find her. Triflin' ass. And this punk is here holding her up, making sure that she not locked up in a loony bin when your ass wants to run off and pretend to be a musician."

LeRoi jumped in Gabriel's face. "Fuck you."

"You ain't man enough for this, honey. And I don't want it. Go on. Get from up here. She is better off without you."

LeRoi chuckled to himself. "What you know about being a man? Tell Virginia I'm looking for her."

"Like I said, I ain't telling her shit. You left her. You find her."

Portia knew this: LeRoi was headed back to Virginia when he walked out her door. So, she lay in her bed for three days and replayed over in her mind the betrayal that she wasn't prepared for. Five years ago in 1978, Portia saw him walk into the Low Down with his arms wrapped around Virginia, the woman who she let live with her when she first moved here from California. Her stomach did flips because this was the first time that she had seen him with someone that she knew. The other women didn't matter. How could they? To Portia, they were nameless, faceless women with breasts and legs that spread like softened butter. They didn't matter to Portia because she couldn't name them, couldn't hate them for having their arms wrapped around his waist while he nibbled on the back of their ears. Anger needs a target, and in order for the target to exist, one has to know its name.

Oh, she was angry, but couldn't place it on the nameless, faceless women, even though she knew what they looked like: one was as tall as a rail with short black hair that made her look more manly than him, another was the color of cooked peaches with red hair from a Clairol box, another had legs that wrapped around him every time they sat in the booth and had dark brown curls that matched her cinnamon skin. Portia could even recite the things that they wore if anyone ever asked her. But the anger she couldn't place on them; the anger didn't have direction, focus. The only thing that she could have said when she saw LeRoi with those nameless, faceless women was, "What is so-and-so doing with *my* man?" or "What is she doing swimming in his eyes?" But even that wasn't enough because there was no power, no heat, and no weight on the *she* simply because Portia didn't know who the *she* was.

So when LeRoi walked in with Virginia—who she learned of from her cousin Rachel and who slept on her couch (fingers always tangled in her hair) many years ago— wrapped around him like the other nameless, faceless women, her stomach flipped, and her skin started to burn. The anger that had floated around in her mind coursed its way to her heart, then back up her throat, and sat on the edges of her lips—it found a target, the opening that it needed, and before she could catch herself, before she could cover her mouth to stop the "O" that her mouth was determined to make, before the tip of her tongue could slide itself over her teeth, it slipped out of her mouth: "Why is that bitch Virginia with my man?"

Portia loved LeRoi before she saw him with Virginia in 1978. Way before the nameless, faceless women. But she also knew that he loved Virginia enough to return back to her. She never understood the connection or the hold that Virginia had over him. She never could come up with any concrete reasons as to why Virginia was always his choice. Always. But Portia had seen the tops of mountains in his freckles and knew what Heaven felt like, what it must have felt like when he came to her, fucked her well. She knew Heaven was in those mountaintops, and if she could get a piece, and if he was willing to let her experience it once, twice, then it was enough for her and she knew that Virginia didn't know what to do with Heaven on mountaintops so why should Portia not experience it? Why not take it when he was giving it away? Why not? She didn't owe Virginia anything, even though she took her in for a month while she looked for a place to live. What harm? Portia thought when her cousin called her from California telling her about a black girl quoting Shakespeare... Portia would help her; she would look out for a lost black girl because no one looked out for her when she was a lost black girl...

But what Portia got in return wasn't worth what she had given up. She could only get to Heaven when *he* felt like it, when *he* wanted her to. And it wasn't fair. And Portia hated Virginia for it. But she didn't, no, she couldn't hate LeRoi, for what she knew and recognized was that

LeRoi was what she still wanted and needed—even if he didn't want or need her. And after lying in bed for three days, Portia got up and walked toward St. Clair, toward the woman who took the mountaintops for granted, the woman who played in Heaven whenever she wanted. Portia's anger craved flesh and blood, and as she marched, singularly, down the street, Portia remembered them that night, linked up like grapes on a vine, and as she marched, something in her clicked like the lock to a chest, and the anger flooded out, and she marched to the top of the steps and waited for Virginia.

"Is he here?"

"Is who here?"

"LeRoi. Is he here?"

"He ain't here, Portia. And he ain't coming back either. Go look for him somewhere else."

"Where you hiding him?"

"Gone, girl. I said he ain't here."

"Didn't I mean anything to you, Virginia? First, you took him from me, and then you threw it in my face. And now you hiding him from me." Portia moved closer to Virginia. "I listened to you and those sad-ass stories about wanting to be an actress. About white folks who didn't give a damn about you, about your mama on her knees. You didn't even like yourself, why would they? I let you stay with me because I knew what it felt like. I liked you, V. Dammit! I didn't mean shit to you, did I?" Portia stood there, raking her eyes over Virginia's body. She still couldn't tell what it was that made LeRoi want her and only her. Virginia didn't even look like the same girl, she thought. At least she tried back then, kept that crazy-ass hair in place. She isn't even pretty; she wears mismatched clothes, she doesn't comb her hair, and he still comes to her. Portia looked at her harder, cocked her head to one side to take in more of Virginia, and when she couldn't see anything more special than what she was, Portia got angrier and reached for Virginia, her hands tightening their grip around her neck.

Virginia's body shook like straw, and she was struggling to breathe. And right before she passed out, Gabriel grabbed Portia and pried her fingers from around Virginia's neck. Gabriel dragged Portia down the stairs and threw her out the front door.

There she stood, Portia, her arms stuck at her sides where Gabriel pinned them.

5

After Amos Smith—a Deacon not yet fire-baptized—decided that only women had the luxury of madness, he cracked open his head, built ledges in it, and sat down. These women, he observed, wore their madness like pretty silk scarves, and when they rolled around in the middle of rooms, screaming, people shook their heads and said, "Dang, girl." Not him. When they ran through hallways singing to dead children long ago lost to them, people stood aside and listened to the haphazard melodies, the strained notes. Not him. Their madness was cultivated, supported, made more acute by the sheer acceptance of it—no questions asked; it just was. Not him. Amos had wanted to succumb to the madness and climb inside of himself after years of bitterness at not feeling God's love but knew that would have confirmed what the church board already decided he was. But it was after his wife crawled in her bed and died that Amos decided that he would set himself up on one of the ledges and watch the world move around him.

That was 1970, and although Amos left the world, he functioned well enough in it, and when the doctor told him in 1982 that his lungs were bleeding, he wanted to write to his son. Amos had put it off for a year now, the letter writing. Gabriel disgusted him, and Amos now fully understood the loathing that his own father had for him, the sour saliva that built up with nowhere to go...

Amos coughed into a white handkerchief with gold crosses stitched in each corner and wiped blood from his mouth. His lungs were on fire, and he had to tell himself not to breathe too hard. When he was told that he would be dead within two years, he got on his knees and begged to God—who he felt turned his back on him the moment his father Zachariah Smith did—for healing and forgiveness. When his lungs continued to spit blood, he gave in to the fact that God no longer had any use for him.

Amos had wanted to be a preacher but had no talent for it. There was nothing in his voice that could sway a congregation hungry for a Lord that they believed was preparing for the Rapture. He didn't have the charisma to make the congregation move like he saw Reverend Richards do when he was a boy. Still, Amos tried and studied and read the Word. He longed for God to put the same spirit in him that he saw countless others get when they sat in the church pews. By twenty-five, Amos was almost out of his father's good graces and knew that the only reason that Reverend Alton Richards worked with him was out of respect for his father. Reverend Richards knew what Amos failed to realize: that Northern Negroes would never be able to preach like Southern ones. No real suffering. No idea of how to move the congregation.

Amos sat with Reverend Richards and memorized words that meant absolutely nothing to him to please a man who forgot what it was like to be disappointed. His father's family wasn't born into slavery, and he was one of the few Negroes at the post office—not in the back sorting mail but delivering it. Everything he touched turned to gold, and behind his back, they called him Luck because everything he wanted, he got. Knowing that Amos would never get the Spirit, never feel the thing that they all felt when they heard an anointed man preach, drove the wedge that had begun to divide Amos and his father in 1935 deeper. Knowing that he would never move people from the pulpit, Amos masked his feeling of being left out by becoming a fast and humbled servant of the Lord: a Deacon not yet fire-baptized.

But that was so long ago. He was an old man now. Amos knew without a doubt that he was in this position—wife dead, son gone, never reaching the ministry— because of what he did when he walked into his bedroom seeing his only son sitting at his wife's vanity table in full makeup. Amos walked over to him, and before he realized it, he slapped his son across the room. He stood over him, his hands shaking, trying to find somewhere for them to be—in his pocket, fondling some keys, wrapped around a pen, holding up the heavy end of a couch—anywhere but where he wanted them to be: around the throat of his son. That was when Amos really knew that God had not ordered his step in His favor.

That day, after he left his wife alone with his son, he sat in the vestibule waiting for a sign, something to assure him that what he saw, what he wanted to kill, wasn't of his doing. Amos knew that he wasn't the best father; maybe too strict, maybe not letting the boy do anything but go to church and Bible study and home was too much. He wasn't that bad, was he? He never hugged the boy or showed him any affection because his father never did. Gabriel was sitting there, all those colors on a face too pretty for a boy. Fine hairs covered cheekbones that Amos knew would make people — women and men — stop in their tracks. Amos whispered, "God, tell me something," and lowered his head.

Amos was supposed to preach this evening, a practice for the real thing, and he couldn't even walk into the sanctuary. He was so shook that the words on the pages made no sense. Amos took a few deep breaths, and a slight nausea took over him as he thought about his ailing father and the love that he would never get. Amos gave up on the respect years ago. But the love, he still held hope for. This would definitely be it — his grandchild in full makeup — the thing to push them further apart. His father's dark, disapproving eyes like mirrors, the white hair so white that you smiled to keep from crying, the beauty of it breathtaking. The air of superiority that his father had was never Amos's to breathe and this last thing, a boy too pretty to be a boy with all those colors on his face. "Lord, is this what I'm supposed to bear?"

"He never gives you more than you can handle." Reverend Richards stood in front of Amos. The disappointment in his eyes wasn't as hurtful as his father's, but it still stung.

"It feels like I can't, Rev."

"Why aren't you preparing for your sermon? Big time for you."

"My mind isn't here."

"Is it ever?" Richards clasped his hands across his stomach.

"How do you wrestle with demons? The ones in your house, the ones that you don't see coming?"

"You do like Christ, son. Wrestle it to the ground and rebuke it!"

"Rebuke it, huh?" Amos played with the cover of his Bible, then ran his finger over the words on his yellow notepad.

"If you can't control the demons in your own house, how can you help others control their demons, son? How can you stand before them, the people who need you to be their bridge to the Lord, and tell them about righteousness?"

"It's too much, you don't know."

"God knows, son! And he knows who can handle it. He knows who to entrust with his flock." Richards placed his hand on Amos's shoulder. He massaged it lightly. "Are you ready to do what you have to do?"

Amos couldn't rebuke that demon and never did his sermon. All he could think of was all that foolishness with makeup and his boy, the fear and paranoia it caused, and the inability to get the Holy Ghost Spirit. His dissension was gradual at first, ignoring a voice that was right in front of him: "Deacon Smith. You hear me?" Dropping things that were just handed to him: church bulletins to proofread, folded money from the Sunday offering, church fans that needed staples. At times, he would be mid-prayer (in front of the pulpit, not behind it) and stop and pat his head—wondering if anyone saw him leave, if anyone knew that he had climbed inside.

The chasm grew larger as his son became more of what he is today. Walking down the street seeing Gabriel in a skirt made it much easier for Amos to slip in and close it up. When his wife died of a broken heart because she saw Gabriel marching with his legs as high and beautiful as the majorettes at Collinwood High School, the chasm swallowed him, and he could do nothing but sit and watch the world move without him. But now he had to rely on a son who he hated more than his father because God chose to finally give up on him.

"Thurman, please bring me some water," Amos said to the young man who now stood in his doorway.

"Here you go, Deacon."

"Thank you, son." Amos took the glass and drank from it slowly. The water wasn't refreshing, but he needed it to calm the boiling. "I need you to go to Cleveland."

"Cleveland?"

"I need you to deliver something for me."

Thurman looked at the old man who had become like a father to him. The sagging skin around his face was ashen, and his fingers were as thin as blades of grass. The sickness was almost unbearable, but Thurman tried to put it out of his head each time he came there. Small chores—sweeping, keeping the grass cut, moving furniture—helped take his mind off the smell that dying brought. "When do you want me to leave?"

"As soon as possible. I don't have a lot of time, son."

Thurman reached for the empty glass and cradled it close to his chest. "Don't say that, Deacon. You look like you have a few more rounds in you."

"Thank you for your kindness. Sit down, son. Let me talk to you. Let me tell you a story."

Thurman sat in the fold out chair directly across from Amos and cracked his knuckles.

"I stopped loving my father because I thought that he stopped loving me. Before that, I loved my father with all I had. But it wasn't good enough. I always felt second-rate with my father. He was a bear of a man, tall like Samson, his favorite man in the Bible. He was a thinking man, didn't come from slavery and so proud of it because he knew wasn't nothing a white man or a newly freed black man could tell him. Freedom wasn't something that he had thought about; it was something that just was for him. I used to sit in awe and watch him rub his chin and nod his head when people would come to our house and talk with him. He was a thinking man and would not be rushed in his answer. I would sit at his side, listening with my eyes and mind, thinking that I could be, should be, like him when I got older. One thing my father liked more than Samson was the men who were called to preach. My father had a great respect for preachers. He thought that anything touched by God was worth following and listening to. To him, a man coated in the blood of Christ was one you wanted on your side at all times."

Amos reached for the Bible that sat in front of him and opened it to where he placed the bookmark with a serious-faced Jesus on it. He traced the wavy pattern of Jesus' hair with his index finger and sighed. "My father loved God, son—loved him so much that there wasn't anything that anyone could do to shake his faith. I know that he wanted me to have that same type of love for God that he did. He would watch me, son, would leave handwritten scriptures lying around the house. I would read them and study them, but they did nothing for me. If anything, they scared me. Made me fear that type of love that made his faith unshakeable. One day, he stood watching me, and he didn't say anything for a long period of time. He then said to me, 'Son, always love God first, then yourself. It will always save you.'

"I looked at him and wondered what I needed to be saved from. And as I got older, I wrestled with what I needed saving from. Telling a kid that God is going to save him without telling him from *what* is enough to rock anyone's world. I tried to think of what it could be: was I going to die young? Would I be walking down the street and fall into a pothole? Would I be slicing carrots for my mother and slice off one of my fingers? I didn't know and couldn't think of what God would need to save me from. I jumped at every sound, looked around every corner, and one day my father was at the bottom of our steps and scared me so that the blood drained out of my face. He looked at me and said, 'What you jumping for?'

"I wasn't sure what to say, so I looked at my trembling hands and said, 'Nothing, Daddy. It's nothing.'

"He walked past me up the stairs, and I watched his back, and before his foot touched the third step, he turned around and said, 'You know that Bible on the mantle? Been saving it for you, been waiting on the right time.' He paused like he always did before he went on: 'I think it's time for you to learn God.'

"I walked over to the mantle and rubbed the big black Bible that had been passed down in our family. The edges of it were curled up, and the black had faded spots on it. My hands trembled even more, and before I picked it up, I thought, Is this what I need saving from? Myself? Is that what my father meant? I grabbed the Bible and hugged it to my chest, finally feeling that I knew what my father did: God was going to save me.

"I was fifteen then and so happy and anxious at the same time. I held on to the Bible and read it every day after school. I flipped through its flimsy pages, afraid that I would ruin it, and my stomach tingled each time that I opened it because I was happy that it had been passed on to me. I worked my way from the beginning to the end. But nothing happened. Nothing I read moved me. Nothing I read made me feel what God was saying. It scared me more than the unknown thing that I had been scared of before. I was afraid because no matter how many times I read and reread Deuteronomy or II Corinthians or Romans, nothing sparked. I knew from watching how Reverend Richards danced around the church that I should be feeling something. But I felt nothing, and so I carried the Bible with me, my finger always saving my spot. I carried it with me in the hopes that maybe the words would magically speak to me. Give me a sign that I was truly the one that God was going to save.

"I came home from school one day, and my father and Reverend Richards were standing on our porch. They were in deep conversation when I walked up, and I lowered my eyes, said, 'Hello,' and tried to walk past them. My father grabbed the tip of my elbow and turned me around so that I was facing him and the Reverend.

"'I been telling the good Reverend here how you won't go nowhere without that Bible. Day and night I see you and it make me proud, son. Real proud.'

"I shifted my weight from one leg to another.

"'What's wrong with you, boy? You can't hold your water for a few minutes?'

"'You know how these young boys are,' said the Reverend. 'Can't hold much these days!'

"Thinking back on it now, Richards regarded me with as much compassion as a cat to a half-dead mouse. He played with me not because he wanted to, but out of necessity. I could hear the resentment in his voice.

"'Well, he needs to hold still for this. Like I said boy, I been telling the Reverend how you carry your Bible day in and day out. I told him that God spoke to you.'

"I opened my mouth to protest, to tell them that God had not spoken to me. That God had been ignoring me. My father put his hand up and silenced me.

"'Now, son, you don't have to tell us what God said to

you because we know it was the right thing. But I am proud that the Lord has seen fit to make you one of his foot soldiers. I have asked Reverend Richards to school you. To help you become a preacher. Preach like they do down south. Like Reverend does here.'

"Reverend Richards looked past me and smiled a crooked smile that made his face seem longer. He talked at me from the side of his mouth. 'We start in the morning. Bring a pad and some paper along with your Bible.'

"I stood there looking at Reverend Richards trying to see if he saw through me, if he knew that the words in the Bible did nothing for me. In my room, I got on my knees and closed my eyes. I asked God to please do something. Please let me feel what I knew that I should feel. I asked him to open me up, use me, and do anything that he needed to, but let me be able to feel.

"The next morning I was sitting in front of the Reverend. Behind him was a big, wooden framed picture of Jesus nailed to the cross, his eyes weeping and looking dead at me. On the wall directly across from the picture was a black grandfather clock. It ticked loudly.

"'Do you know what your name means?'

"I turned from the weeping eyes and looked at him. 'No.'

"'It means burden. Are you prepared to carry the burden? Most people say that God spoke to them and told them that they are ready to carry the burden of His blood. Are you ready to do that, Amos? Are you ready to carry that burden? Son, it's a heavy load. So much so that it breaks men, son, reduces them to ashes. It's not something that people who are armed and prepared for the burden take lightly. When your father came to me and told me, I was skeptical. And I hope that you can understand. It's not because I don't like you, son. No, you shouldn't mistake my disturbance as me not liking you. That has nothing to do with it. It's just that people like me, people who have *really* talked to God and have accepted what He has asked us to do—because it really is a burden, son—know how hard it is to lead a flock of non-believers. Oh, yes, son, yes—we have a whole house of those who believe in His mercy, in His love. But the real challenge, the real burden, you see, is getting those who reside outside of our house to come in and love the Lord as we do. So, it's necessary for me to sit down with you and make sure that you have the back to carry that burden, son. So, understand that you will be tested, son, and not by me, but by God. Because God is the only one that can truly judge what's in your heart.'

"He was leaning so close to me that I could smell the peppermint that had been in his mouth. He looked at me waiting on me to answer. Waiting on me to tell him that I was ready to carry the burden. That I was ready to be a foot soldier of the Lord." Amos broke into a fit of coughing and had to double over until it stopped.

"Are you okay, Deacon? Don't move; let me get some more water." Thurman stood up to leave.

"No, I am fine." Amos sat up straight and palmed the Bible. It was the same one from his childhood, and it pained him slightly that it wouldn't be passed down to his son. "It's just hard thinking about never getting the chance to preach my sermon and the constant disappointment that

I am to God and my father. I need you to take this letter to Gabriel."

"Gabriel?" Thurman looked at the Deacon, then dropped his eyes. "I didn't know that you knew where he was."

Amos stroked the envelope. He didn't respond to the accusation in the question. "Give it to him." Amos handed the letter to Thurman. "And don't answer any of his questions. Promise me, son. Promise me that you won't tell him anything about me."

"I promise, Deacon."

"I don't want him coming back to Pittsburgh for me. I'm not long in this world. I just pray that God forgives me." Amos handed the Bible to Thurman. "Here, I want you to have this."

Church, I want you all to know that the Hell we been fighting against with Fire and Brimstone is right outside these doors. Right outside these doors that hold so much of what we believe in, so much that we live by, the word of our Lord and Savior, Jesus Christ. Amen?

Amen!

You see, we have a battle to prepare for. A battle with Satan, once himself among the Chosen, but one who decided that God's Love and Mercy was too kind—yes, too kind, children—for he rebuked it with his own filthy mouth, told God that he didn't want His love, a love that we work for everyday, children. Amen?

Amen!

Told God that His only Son meant nothing to him. Curled up his body like the rattling snake, to twist and turn anyone who would be taken from Christ into believing that God's Love wasn't real. Amen. And so, children, we are on the battleground. It's right outside our doors. And what do we do? Amen, Church. What do we do, Church, for those who have listened to the slippery tongue of Satan? What do we tell them, children?

What do we tell them, Preacher?

Will they listen, Pastor?

Amen.

Amen, children, we have to show them the goodness in God's Love. Show them the mercy of God's Love. Show them the forgiving arms of His Love. Show them the God that we see in our everyday walk. Amen? But we can't mislead the flock, children, can't show them just the good side of God and not tell them the whole story. Amen? They need to also know that my God is a wrathful God. A God that has two swords, amen. Church, we have to lead them back to us. Lead them away from the filthy juke joints that line our city streets. The bodies that consume themselves each time they swallow that poison. Amen. Lead our lost daughters back to us. Lead them back from the streets; stop them from letting our lost sons swallow them whole. We need to bring them all back to these doors, Church, back to a home that is forgiving if they openly confess their sins. Willingly let go of Satan and the hold he has on them. Rebuke him in the name of Jesus. Lord! If You can calm a raging sea, still the murky waters. Lord! Save us from the Devil and his magic. Church, we have to save our flock. Save our doors. But before we do that, Saints, let's take a trip.

Praise God!

Let's take a trip with Paul the Apostle. Let's take a trip with his family. Let's put on our armor, put on our Coat of

Righteousness, and take that trip with Paul. Only our trip won't be to Rome, children.

Where are we going, Pastor?

Family, we are going to take a trip right outside of our doors. That's our Rome, you see? You see, Church, Rome is right outside our door, and we are watching it happen. So, we have to take a trip. Take a journey into the filth that has become the way of life here. Paul turned his back on God, amen?

Amen!

Tell us why Paul turned his back on God?

What he learn, Pastor? What he learn?

Children, not only will I tell you why he turned away, but I will also tell you what he learned. Paul was a non-believer, Church. Everywhere he went, he talked against Christianity. He watched executions, amen. And relished in it. Amen. And then one day, one glorious day, on his way to Damascus—yes, sweet, sweet Damascus—he was blinded by the Glory of God… Vision wiped out by the fingertips of God. One minute he saw, family, and the next, it was taken from him. Amen.

Praise God!

Lord, have Mercy on Paul. Sweet Mercy!

Three days. Three days, he sat in darkness. Sat in the darkness of his thoughts. Left to ponder the Love and Glory of God. Then with the instructions of God, Ananias of Damascus restored his sight. Gave him what only He could take away. See, children, those who dwell outside of the arms of the Lord don't know God's Love. Don't know how far His hands reach. Don't know how strong the palms of His hands are, my children. Strong palms that hold us all in His hands, hands that made the light and the dark. Made the heavens and the earth. Made the wind and the seas. My children, you see. But they are blind. They are blind but walk the earth as if they see. As if their sight is clear, free of the debris that clouds their eyes. They see not what He is; they see not what He does. He has placed them there, blinded them, so that they can see within themselves—see His Glory, see what is right in front of them

What is it, Pastor? What is it that they cannot see?

Sister Pearl, they can't see Him for trying to see past Him. They want to thank some man for giving them the extra pennies to buy that smoked hock, for providing that extra bag of rice; they thank them silently in their heads—thank people—white men, white women at the welfare office, the white people who they scrub floors for—for what they are able to get. See, Brother Charles, yes, listen to me, hear me they they they don't know that the Lord is the one who has provided for them. The Lord is thy Shepherd, Sister Kay, the Lord, and they are blinded and He wants them to see. And you know, Sister Clarice, it's as much our fault as it is theirs. If we don't help lead them, help them see the light, see the true and sweet and beautiful and bountiful—you hear me, Congregation?

Amen!

Praise God in all His Glory!

My God, my God!

Yes, children, praise Him, for He is come! Oh Lord, forgive us for not leading them to the Light! Lord, forgive us for allowing our brothers and sisters to be blinded all the day long! Oh, Lord, put it in our hearts and in our minds to bring those blinded, wounded, lost, confuuuused sheep, yes Lord, confuussed sheep back to the pasture. See, children, we have to go on a journey. We have to strap up our shoes, put on our armor for Christ, and begin to bring them back to His arms. Oh yes, *children! Oh yes! We can no longer afford to put this journey off much longer; we can no longer sit in His house, feed off of His loaves and fishes and not share His love; we can no longer afford to be bystanders in the war for people's souls. The Devil is a liar, children. A stone-cold liar—so cold, children, so cold—and we have to unleash them, bind the Devil—bind him, bind him in the name of Jesus, bind him! And so, children, as Paul was brought back to the light, and as Paul went on his journey to spread the words and open the eyes of those who chose to be blinded to Christ's word, to the Son of God, He calls us soldiers, and we have to strap up, roll up our sleeves, and prepare for war!*

6

"Do you know who that is across the street?" Mrs. Lee asked Gabriel.

Gabriel walked to the window and stood beside Mrs. Lee. "If we didn't have all of these damn prison bars then I might be able to tell you. Plus, I don't have on my glasses."

"You're safe, aren't you?" Lee looked up at Gabriel.

"Uh huh."

"Well, then. He's been standing there for about an hour now. Go find out who he is."

Gabriel squinted and leaned in closer to the window. From what he could tell, the man was as tall as he was and the color of cinnamon. The cinnamon man stood stock-still. Gabriel sucked his teeth and walked back to the counter. "Let him stand there. He looks content."

Mrs. Lee rolled her eyes and went to the door. She opened it and waved to the man. He didn't move at first, but when she waved to him harder, he looked both ways, and then crossed the street toward her. She held the door open with her leg, and when the man got closer, Mrs. Lee let the door close behind her and stood in front of it.

"You lost?" she asked as she looked him up and down. He wore a tan suit that hung slightly off of him; in the front left pocket was a light blue handkerchief with brown polka dots. As he stood in front of her, he held a brown fedora. His hairline was receding but he had a boyish face.

"I'm looking for someone."

"I'm sure you won't find them standing in front of the rink." Mrs. Lee looked past him, then looked at his shoes. "Nice shoes. Who are you looking for?"

"I was told that he lived here, and I was waiting on him to walk out the door."

"Who are you looking for?"

"Gabriel Smith."

Lee looked him over again and straightened out the pleats in her rosemary-colored skirt. "What you want with him?"

"I have something for him."

The clothes weren't that fancy but he wasn't a slob either. The shoes — Stacy Adams — were spotless. "I will give it to him."

He shifted his weight from one foot to another, and a look of concern spread across his face as wrinkles appeared in his forehead. "I have strict instructions."

"Are you the police?"

"No. Do you know him?"

"What is your name?"

"Thurman Bridge. Can you tell me where he is?"

"Whatever you need to get to him, I can take it."

"I told you, ma'am, that I have to give it to him myself."

"Give me what?" Gabriel had come around from the back. "Give me what?"

Thurman turned his head and stopped on the face. He saw something familiar but couldn't put his finger on it. The angles on the face were beautiful, yet masculine. The eyes were hidden beneath blue eyeshadow, but they were familiar—they danced over him, making him uncomfortable and hot at the same time. "I am looking for Gabriel Smith."

Gabriel's eyes squinted at hearing his full name. He didn't know this man and wondered who he was and where he came from. He hesitated, then spoke slowly. "I'm Gabriel Smith, but I haven't been called that in a long time."

Thurman lowered his eyes and began to stammer. "I...I...I..."

"Come on, child, spit it out."

Thurman, embarrassed, had to regroup.

"Do you want me to call the police?" Mrs. Lee said as she moved closer to Gabriel.

"Hush, old woman. You always trying to call the police on somebody. This man can't even talk. He ain't gon' do nothing."

"I'm sorry. I heard that you..."

"I heard it, too. But it ain't true, trust me!" Gabriel broke into laugher. "Do I know you?"

"I did before..." Thurman caught himself. The young man he had fallen in love with was standing before him in full makeup. He was breathtaking, and he wondered if

Gabriel looked the same without makeup. He wanted to reach out his hand and touch the high cheekbones, but caught himself.

"You did before what?"

"We grew up together. You didn't talk to me, but I knew you."

Gabriel looked away at the reminder of Pittsburgh and his mother and father. He still kept the bus ticket tucked away, but he didn't want to revisit the reason behind the leaving. "I'm not that Gabriel, so you can stop standing across the street and go on home."

"Your father sent me. Deacon Amos Smith."

Gabriel looked at him and shook his head. "Like I said, I'm not that Gabriel anymore." He walked back towards the store.

"I have a letter from him."

Gabriel stopped, and his body trembled. He then turned around and faced the cinnamon-colored man who could only have been sent by the one person who he simultaneously hated and loved. Gabriel stared at him longer. "What is your name?"

"Thurman Bridge."

Gabriel stretched out a hand to him. "Gabriel Smith. But everyone calls me Butterfly Lady. I'm cooking dinner tonight. Come back at eight. I live in 201." Gabriel turned and walked back into the store.

Inside the hotel room, Thurman removed his jacket. He hung it from the leg of the hotel chair, then opened the small window so that air could circulate in the stuffy room. He sighed. The letter, in its smallness, had been heavy. It was just as heavy as the sickness that he encountered everyday with the Deacon, as heavy as the memory of his strangled sister, and now, just as blunt as the realization that what they said in the Hill District was true: Gabriel had made himself a woman. Thurman lay across the bed so that his legs dangled over the edge. He had gotten the address from the Deacon, and when he finally made it to the store—after catching the Number 3 bus in front of the hotel, then transferring to the Number 1 bus—he didn't know if he should go knock on the door or wait. So, he waited across the street to see if Gabriel would walk out the front door. He hadn't seen him in years, but he still remembered, he thought, the boy he had fallen in love with. But when he saw two women—one with French braids that parted her face, the other abnormally tall but thin—walk out of the door, he continued to wait. Thurman sat up and rested his head in his hands. He was supposed to hand him the letter, leave, and get right back on the bus to Pittsburgh. But when he realized that Gabriel was the tall, thin woman, he couldn't move. He couldn't leave; he had to find out the story behind the deep blue eyeshadow, the reasoning behind the long skirt that touched Gabriel's ankles, the wrist as thin as violin strings. He had forgotten about the letter, had forgotten the mission and the man that gave it to him.

Thurman walked to the chair and pulled the letter out of his coat pocket. He opened the nightstand and found a Bible. The letters were faded, and the cover was cracked like dry skin. Thurman placed the letter in the Bible, put it back into the nightstand drawer, and closed it. Just like that, he had disobeyed the man who had saved him from himself. Just like that, he had decided that Gabriel was more important to him than the Deacon. Thurman sat back on the bed and remembered the healthy Deacon Smith who watched him with solemn eyes at his strangled sister's funeral. The word *"strangled"* was what he remembered most about his sister's death, and the pink satin lining of her coffin. It was all over the news, the newspapers, the tongues and lips of people in Pittsburgh: black secretary strangled by her boss, her lover. Everywhere Thurman went in the neighborhood, people's eyes followed him, and when he looked up at them, they wouldn't look away—they shook their heads. What he couldn't figure out was whether it was out of pity or shame.

The day of his sister's funeral, Thurman sat at the back of the church, his black suit slack on his body, and tapped his foot seven times, then started all over again. He figured if he did it enough times, then the service would be over. When he looked toward the front, he saw his sister's hair, and knew that she, Nina Bridge, would have been upset with such tight curls around her face. He then looked at the mourners; everyone was crying except for Deacon Smith. He just stared at Thurman. Thurman tried to look back at the tight curls of his sister, but he was drawn back to the Deacon, and the Deacon's eyes never left his. If his mother hadn't screamed, "Lord, have mercy, Lord!" then they would have been transfixed forever. After the funeral, Thurman sat in a folding chair in the corner of the kitchen.

From there, he could see people surrounding his mother like she was honey; he wondered if she was suffocating as much as he was. Did she want to scream until there was no air left in her lungs, like he? Did his mother even realize that her child, his sister, was never going to walk back through the front door, never stand in this kitchen, on this aging, broken tile, and stir pots of oatmeal, snap fresh green beans, shred cheese for baked macaroni? Did she know, like he did, that death didn't just take one life, but that it took everything around it, emptied everything out, and left only the shell? Did she? He thought about this as he watched the people rub his mother's back, offering her a plate or a glass of ginger ale to settle her stomach. Thurman looked down, and he felt the eyes on him again.

"How are you holding up, son?"

Thurman didn't say anything.

"I know about death, too. It can swallow you without you knowing it. I lost my wife, and, my son, well—he may as well be dead. If you want to talk, I am here to listen."

Thurman looked into the eyes of Deacon Smith, and then watched him as he walked away and out the front door.

A week later, Thurman stood on the front porch of the Deacon's house, and before he could ring the bell, the door opened.

"Come in."

Thurman walked in slowly and stood aside as Amos closed the front door.

"We can sit in the living room. Don't use it much since Mattie, but it's still a nice enough place. Water?"

"Yes, please." Thurman sat on a green couch. It felt like he was being sucked in, so he pulled himself up and sat, pensively, on the edge of the cushion.

"Here." Amos handed Thurman the glass. "I was wondering when you would come."

Thurman took a sip of water; the condensation fogged up the glass. "I wondered, too."

"What did *you* wonder?" Amos stood over him, and it made him nervous.

"I wondered why she had to be killed." Thurman looked up at Amos and then shrugged his shoulders. "But then, I thought, what's the use in wondering when the answer is right there?"

"Without wonder, there would be no reason to think."

"Thinking hurts, Deacon."

"It also heals."

"Has it healed you?"

Amos opened his mouth to speak, but nothing came out. He had been the one to counsel, if half-heartedly, people about grief, loss, crumbling marriages, and ways to save their souls. But no one ever made him think about how to heal himself, how to save his soul. God had abandoned him, so he put everybody else in the abandoning category.

"Well, son. I don't know."

Thurman drank more of the water and then ran his index finger along the rim of the glass. "At my house, after the funeral, I was thinking of what anyone could possibly say to my mother to make her feel better. What words could they say to stop her from always remembering her child in a box lined in pink satin? I couldn't think of one word, you know, because I knew that if I couldn't find any words, how could they. I can't ever tell myself anything. All I can pull out of me is *"strangled."* Thurman sat the glass down, then picked it up again and raised it to his lips before putting it down again. "You were the only one not crying."

"When you get to be my age, grief becomes your friend. When you see and talk to as many people as I do, misery lingers without effect. You learn to live with it, son."

"Where is he?"

"Who?"

"Your son."

Amos walked to the end of the living room where the mantel was. On it was a picture of Mattie. She was smiling, doing something with her hands. What, he couldn't see, because the picture had faded spots where the oil from his fingers had invaded. She was happy before Gabriel started marching with butterflies on his head and doing full scissor kicks up and down McClarren. Everyone on The Hill, everyone in Allegheny County talked about his son, his boy; everyone talked about Amos, he suspected, about his inability to shore up his home, his inability to be fire-baptized. Amos brought the picture closer to his face. There was a sudden urge to see what Mattie was doing with her hands, a need to see what was making her so happy. He stared closer, harder, and when he realized that she was holding Gabriel's hand, he placed the picture back on the mantel and turned back towards Thurman. "I don't know where he is. He killed my wife; therefore, he killed me."

After that first encounter with Deacon, Thurman kept coming back and kept asking him about Gabriel. When he realized that the Deacon wasn't going to tell him, "Son, let it go," he just sat and listened to the Deacon talk about his desire to be a preacher and how that was broken for him. Most times, Thurman would pick up the broom and sweep the wood floors while Amos talked; other times he would trim the yard while Amos watched. The buzzing people stopped coming by his house. His mother sat in their foyer from the moment sunlight hit her cherry-colored skin until the moon made the silver in her hair sparkle. Thurman would walk past her on his way to the Deacon's, and she would be there when he got back. He stopped asking her how her day was because the answer became the same, automatic, "In the Bye and Bye, child. In the Bye and Bye."

He would tell Amos about his mother, and Amos would look at him and say, "Let her be. Her grief is her own."

Thurman had been coming and going to Amos's house for over fifteen years when he found out that the Deacon was sick and knew, indeed, where his son was. When the Deacon called him into his office and asked him to take the letter to Gabriel, he felt his heart skip a beat because he had pushed Gabriel to the back of his mind like he did his sister's death and his sitting mother. When they were both boys, Thurman couldn't love Gabriel, openly. Now, maybe he could tell him what he felt for him all those years ago. After he swore to Amos that he would deliver the letter and come right back to Pittsburgh, he realized that he didn't have a suitcase.

Thurman knew that he could borrow one from

Deaconess Stewart. While he stood at her door, Thurman played back in his mind the face of the boy and wondered what he looked like as a man. What had stayed with him — the intense eyes like his father's, the high cheekbones — or what had been lost — innocence, freedom, hope — or what had been added — a full beard, loafers, and Oxford shirts. When the Deaconess came to the door, Thurman asked her to borrow a suitcase.

"Taking a trip, huh?" Deaconess Stewart had on a cream housedress with embroidered roses on the pockets. She turned her head up at him, waiting for an answer.

"Yes, ma'am. Just a quick trip to Cleveland."

"You ever been to Cleveland?"

"No, ma'am."

"Huh." She stuffed her hand in her right pocket and pulled out a mint. "You want a peppermint?"

"No. I have to get going, Deaconess Stewart. When I come back, I will cut your yard."

"I sure do appreciate it, Thurman. You be careful in Cleveland. I heard it was rough. Come in while I go get it."

"Yes, ma'am."

Thurman watched her as she made her way up the stairs. He heard her shuffling and moving stuff around. As he waited, Thurman didn't know if he should be mad at the Deacon or happy. He hadn't realized how much he wanted to find Gabriel, how much his absence was a part of his everyday life, until he heard his name come out of the Deacon's mouth. He couldn't move then, and he tried to keep the shock and hurt out of his voice as he confirmed that that was who the Deacon wanted him to take the letter to. He wondered if Gabriel would remember him, or would he be the thing, the person that people said that he had become. Thurman caught himself from smiling; there was no use being happy when the outcome was far from certain. He still made a promise, and he intended to keep his word to the Deacon.

When she came back downstairs, she handed him a small, brown suitcase. "This all I got, but you welcome to it."

"Thank you, Deaconess. I have to go."

"Oh, okay. Tell Deacon Smith I said hello, you hear?"

"Yes. I will."

Thurman got off the bed and looked in the mirror. He wished that he had packed something with a little more color, but there wasn't room. Thurman took one of the washcloths and ran hot water on it. He washed his face, cleaned his ears. He wrung the water out of the washcloth and neatly folded it into a square. Thurman took a deep breath and picked up his hat. The letter stayed caressed in the paper arms of the Bible.

Gabriel stood in his kitchen and looked at the rotting tomatoes. He tossed them into the garbage and headed downstairs. He had no idea what made him invite a man he didn't know back to his house for dinner. Sending a letter by an actual person rather than the mail was just like his father: theatrical. "And they call me a Drama Queen," he said out loud to himself. Besides, Amos was the only living relative that he knew of and maybe it was time he reconnected with him. Maybe. Gabriel walked down to the store. Mrs. Lee leaned against the counter.

"What are you still doing here?"

"Waiting on you to steal my food."

"Look, heifer, I don't steal nothing from nobody that they don't want taken."

"You don't pay for it, either."

"I pay enough for everything. You just don't know it."

"Why are you doing this, Gabriel?"

"I need some tomatoes for my spaghetti sauce."

"No." Mrs. Lee walked toward him and grabbed his thin wrist. "I love you. Isn't that enough?"

"What are you talking about, Miss Thing?" Gabriel snatched his wrist away and picked over the small selection of tomatoes.

"He is only going to hurt you."

Gabriel picked up a bright red tomato and squeezed it. It was firm. He did it to another and then balanced them in the palm of his right hand and forearm. "I have been hurt enough. What is he going to do to me? I killed my mother, and my father killed me off in his head."

"Stop that nonsense. You did not kill your mother." Lee took one of the tomatoes out of Gabriel's hand and thumped it. "Too ripe. Pick another one." She then bit into it.

"It may be nonsense, but it's the only sense that I have to go by. There isn't anything that he can tell me that will send me back to Pittsburgh, if that's what you are worried about."

"It's more than Pittsburgh. He didn't even know who

you were. He couldn't even speak when he realized that it was you."

"I couldn't help that… When he said my father's name, it felt like something was cracking in me… I wanted it to stop, so I invited him over to dinner."

"That's your solution? A spaghetti dinner?"

"Do you have any other?" Gabriel said.

"Butterfly Lady," said Mrs. Lee. You told him your name was Butterfly Lady."

"That's my name."

"Who still calls you that? Who will he really be talking to?"

"Look, if he wants to talk to me, then he has to talk to *all* of me!" Gabriel spread his arms out. "This is who I am."

"Is it really?"

Gabriel turned his back to her and picked another tomato. When he turned back around, the tomato in Lee's hand was dripping; the juice ran down her arm like she had an open wound. "Who am I, then?"

Lee bit into the tomato and chewed slowly. "I don't think it's a good idea to open closed doors when you know why you closed them in the first place."

Gabriel watched her throw the tomato in the garbage. She wiped the juice onto her skirt—the only one she wore—and picked at something in her teeth with her tongue. "I can take care of myself. I have survived all this time, haven't I?"

"You're always surviving."

"I have to go. Don't stay here too late."

He walked up the back stairs to his apartment and leaned his ear against Virginia's door. He wondered where Chance was. When he turned to leave, he heard soft sobs and shook his head. This is why he didn't carry stuff with him; this is why he wasn't afraid of being hurt by the cinnamon colored man: there was nothing left to hurt.

He turned on the pot to boil the noodles and took the ground beef out of the refrigerator. While the water boiled, he seasoned the beef with black pepper, salt, garlic, and red pepper flakes. He added olive oil to the beef and turned the fire on; the meat began to sizzle. He cut up an onion and both tomatoes. Gabriel added tomato paste and two cups of water. The meat sauce simmered, and then he placed the noodles into the boiling water. He tasted the sauce from the tip of a wooden spoon—it needed more salt. Gabriel then reached for the loaf of Wonder Bread on top of the refrigerator. He spread butter on four slices, sprinkled garlic powder on them, and placed them on a worn cookie sheet. He slid them in the oven, then drained the pasta. Once everything was done, he sat at the vanity with a glass of wine. He touched the photo of his mother and stroked her face. "Well, Mama, let it begin." And he swallowed the wine in one gulp as he waited for the cinnamon-colored man.

Gabriel was on his second glass of Riesling when he heard a knock at the door. He was still seated at the vanity, and before he got up to answer, he checked his makeup in the bright lights of the mirror. He answered the door, one arm holding it open and the other lounged across the doorjamb. "Welcome to my humble abode." He stepped aside and watched Thurman walk in. "Here, let me show you around. Here is my couch—I don't use it much, but when I do, it is comfortable. There is my kitchen—a bit small—but a girl does what she can with it. On the other side of that wall is my bedroom, and next to it, my bathroom. That's it. Now, you are familiar and no longer a guest." Gabriel waved his hand to the couch and Thurman sat down. "Wine?"

"I don't drink."

"I guess you do know my father." Gabriel laughed then took a sip. "What do you do for fun, sir?"

"I work around your house and help other people at the church."

"My house? It ain't been my house in quite some time." Gabriel smiled to himself. "Cleaning up? Ain't you the saint? I guess you're the apple of his eye."

Gabriel went into the kitchen and stirred the simmering sauce. He called out to Thurman, "I hope you like spaghetti... My mama loved spaghetti. She could make a mean sauce. Your mama make homemade sauce?" Gabriel now stood in the doorway and stared at Thurman.

"My mother is dead, but when she was alive, she could make anything."

Gabriel saw the same affection that he had for his mother in Thurman's face, the way the creases around his eyes softened when he talked about her, the slight tremble in his bottom lip. "You loved your mother, huh?"

"I did." Thurman watched Gabriel move from one end

to the other. It was almost as if the apartment was made to the specifications of Gabriel's stride, the exactness making it possible for him to appear to be floating. "I am sorry about your mother."

Gabriel sat down next to Thurman and held the glass close to his face and studied it. "Why are you sorry? Did you know her?"

"No. But Deacon Smith talks about her all the time. He loved her."

"That man didn't love nothing but the sound of his voice. He used to walk around the house with a faded yellow notepad, reading out loud to himself, annoying the hell out of my mother. She was a good woman, you know. Good to him because she never let on to being bothered by the constant sound of my father's voice. Now me? I loved her." Gabriel took one last sip and jumped up. "Time for a refill."

Thurman followed Gabriel into the kitchen. He watched Gabriel pour another glass. "Maybe you drink too much."

"Maybe you need to mind your own business." Gabriel took a long swallow.

Thurman looked at the thin wrist. "I didn't mean to offend you."

"Well, you are doing a bang-up job." Gabriel laughed and walked past Thurman. When he didn't follow, Gabriel turned back to him and said, "What are you waiting on?"

Thurman blushed and followed Gabriel into the living room.

"So, what you got?"

"Huh?" Thurman hadn't taken his eyes off of Gabriel since he walked into the apartment. He had committed to memory the long lashes that fluttered when Gabriel blinked; the dark lining around the lips; the thin, thin wrists; and the cheekbones high enough for Thurman to sit on. He was too busy replaying those images in his mind to know what Gabriel was talking about.

"You came looking for me, remember? You said my father sent me something. Where is it?"

Thurman looked nervous; he popped his knuckles, a habit he picked up after his sister was killed. "Let's talk."

"Talk?" Gabriel smiled at Thurman. "We talked outside the store."

"Then why did you invite me to dinner if you didn't want to talk?"

"Oh, child, please. I wanted you to stop saying his name."

Thurman couldn't tell if Gabriel was mad or happy. He hesitated. "Why do they call you Butterfly Lady?"

Gabriel looked past Thurman to the vanity. He wanted to reach for the picture of his mother for comfort. He wanted to hold her hand one more time, forget that she left him when she saw him doing what he was born to do. "I danced. Marched, really." Gabriel pushed loose hair behind his ears. "I was a kid, then, you know. I didn't know why I wanted to do those things. I think I just wanted him to pay me some attention. He wanted her to wear makeup all the time. A First-Lady-in-training was what he used to tell her. I wanted some of his attention, but I didn't know how to tell him. He was too busy trying to convince himself and other people that he was meant to be a preacher. It wore him down, you know. And when he caught me, I was trying to get him to see me, to play with me, to read something other than the Bible to me."

Gabriel's voice trailed off, and he swirled the Riesling in the glass; a few drops flew out. "So I started doing it. Started marching and dancing in the streets on The Hill. A girlfriend of mine gave me the butterfly headband and I wore it and danced to "God Bless America." People started calling me the Butterfly Lady, and I liked it, and it has been me. It killed my mother, though. She lay in the bed when she saw me, laid right there and let herself die. I know she loved me, but I also know that she was just as shamefaced as my father." Gabriel sat the glass down and stretched. "I left after she died and ain't going back."

Thurman folded then unfolded his arms. There didn't seem to be any air where he stood. "I'm sorry she died."

"Why are you so sorry? You can tuck your sorry in that Bible I am sure that you keep."

Thurman flinched. He had come here ready to split his heart in two and give Gabriel one half, an assurance of how far he would go for him, and Gabriel seemed primed for an attack. "I can't seem to say the right thing, can I?"

There were flecks of black in the cinnamon-colored face and Gabriel wanted to pick each fleck out, one by one, and smooth it out. "Why did he send you?"

"Because I know you."

"I don't know you."

Gabriel was right. Thurman didn't know him, had never spoken to him. He used to watch the bullies beat

Gabriel up. And he did nothing about it, and for years he felt guilt and underneath that guilt was affection that intensified the helplessness that he felt. It could have been him being tortured, unprotected. "I knew you before...before you were a lady." Thurman looked at Gabriel again and then dropped his eyes. "But you aren't a lady."

Gabriel turned his nose up at Thurman. "I *am* a lady."

"You are a man wearing a dress and makeup."

Gabriel clasped his hands together and rested his chin on his hands. He thought about what Thurman said and shook his head slightly. "See, you have me confused. I am not a man in a dress. I am me."

Thurman chuckled.

"What's so damn funny?" Gabriel's eyelashes jumped as he spoke—moving like the wings of bees.

Thurman held his hands up in mock defeat and walked over to the Victrola. He played with the needle and imagined the hiss and moan of the record as it spun around. "You still play this thing?"

"Do I? I sit right there," Gabriel pointed to the vanity, "and play my records. And when I am really feeling the music, I dance around the room, pretending that my mama and I are dancing beside lost souls. Yes, I play it. And it is grateful." Gabriel pulled a record out of a white sleeve and placed it on the Victrola. The needle caught the groove and a throaty "That's All I Ask" floated in the air. "It's Nina. Come on, do you dance?" Gabriel grabbed Thurman hands and pulled him toward him.

Thurman tried to pull away. "I don't dance."

Gabriel placed Thurman's hands around his waist and started to move slowly. "I won't tell. One dance ain't gon' send you to hell."

Thurman stood stock-still at first. The music rang in his ears. The voice was like soft rain, and he started to move slowly with Gabriel.

"See, I knew you had some rhythm in you." Gabriel cocked his head to one side as if he was trying to catch all of the words, all of the meaning and wonder of the record. "See," Gabriel said as they moved. "She doesn't want much. Doesn't want you to hold the world in your hands, on your shoulders...she just wants love..." Gabriel sighed deeply and his shoulders relaxed. "See, that's all that she asks. That's all that I ask..."

Thurman was self-conscious as he moved. He thought about Deacon and his promise to come right back to Pittsburgh. But how could he not stay with the one person that he felt he could give his heart to, split it right down the middle? Thurman watched Gabriel's head as it dropped to his shoulder, gave in to the music. Gabriel opened his eyes and smiled up at Thurman. And as the notes moved around the room, Thurman leaned down and kissed Gabriel. Gabriel kissed him back, and their tongues explored one another's. This is what Thurman had been waiting for. This was the moment that he had been saving himself for, the reason that he had refused his body the touch and affection of other men. Gabriel. This is what his hunger had been for. Gabriel. Now he could rest a little easier; now, thinking about his sister and the bee people who hovered around his mother would be bearable. Now, he believed, he could protect Gabriel and never leave him vulnerable to pain, to people. Now he knew that the longing and fever that came with love was right here all along and could be extinguished right here. Now he knew that he had a home and a place where he could be fed. And now he knew for certain that the Deacon was wrong, for how could one who loved so hard, so completely, not want others to experience it? As they embraced, Thurman's heart split in two and he was now ready to give Gabriel his half.

7

"It wasn't supposed to be like this, was it?" Mrs. Lee stood on Old Man's porch, her olive skin moist under the porch light.

Old Man was shocked to see her. In all the years that he had known her, he had never seen her away from the store. No one knew where she lived, and there were rumors that she actually slept in the back of her store to save money. Old Man didn't know if what they said around St. Clair was true, but he liked the mystery surrounding her—it endeared her to him, connected them in his mind. "What are you talking about, Lee?" He held the screen door open with two fingers and moved aside.

She stood in the foyer smoothing her skirt and sweeping her feet lightly against the hardwood floor. "These kids... We are supposed to protect them, right?"

"We do the best that we can. The rest is up to them."

She sucked her teeth. "We can't leave it up to them. They will surely lose if we do."

"Haven't we already let them down, then?" Old Man squeezed her shoulders as he limped slowly past her into the living room.

"Where is your cane?"

"It's here. Sometimes, it's a nuisance."

"Hmm..."

Old Man eased down onto the couch. His right hand automatically massaged his bad leg.

"You know," Lee said as she sat across from him, "I should have let you call the police all those years ago."

"Woman," Old Man chuckled, "You 'bout tore my head off when I suggested it. You don't mean that."

"You are right. I don't." She smiled and looked up to the ceiling. "I don't know why he needs other people to love him."

"You want him to only love you?"

"No, but...it's the *need* that scares me... When I looked at him that day, his legs sticking out of that box, his face thin, I saw him, Odell. I saw the thing he was running from—I saw him lose himself every day because no one would love him. I was there... I thought I helped him get over that."

"He ain't telling you to leave, is he?"

"No. But I don't like what I saw today. He invited that man to dinner to stop him from talking. Can you imagine?"

"All men got to eat, Lee."

"Men need to hurt things, too."

Old Man turned from her and looked toward the stairs. He had seen LeRoi and wanted to try and stop him from bouncing all over the place. He also felt bad for lying to

Virginia about not seeing him. "Gabriel can take care of himself."

"I know, but…" Lee hesitated. "Look: that man almost died when he realized that Gabriel wasn't a woman. I felt it then. I felt the hurt coming."

"It will come, Lee." Old Man took her in—the olive skin, the thin lips, the small hands that played with the inside of her thighs, the French braids coming undone at the end. "It will come and when it does, we have to be there to hold them up." Old Man looked at Lee and saw the same fear and wonder and longing for Gabriel that he had for his nephew. "I can't help him either, Lee. I can't get Roi to sit down somewhere, can't get him to treat anything or anyone right but that guitar." Old Man let his head rest on the back of the couch. "It's the music. It makes me nervous, and I'm just listening. I can't imagine being responsible for playing it…"

Mrs. Lee looked at him. "I never understood the music."

They both got quiet; outside, the rumble of cars sounded like people arguing.

"I want them to be better than us, Lee."

Mrs. Lee looked at Old Man and imagined rain falling down his red skin. She wondered if it colored the ground as it fell, if it took pieces of him as it hit the ground. "I want them to survive themselves."

Above her head, Mrs. Lee heard them dancing. And music. Earlier, when she got back to the store, she picked up a broom and started to sweep. Now, she held the broom to her thigh and listened hard to the music. It was loud but muffled, and she leaned her body up to the ceiling as if this would help her make out the words. What's the use? she thought to herself. She never understood this music. Their music. Soul-people music. Music-to-save-their-lives music. Heart-wrenching-sung-from-their-belly music. Dancing-all-night-to-stop-from-crying music. You-ain't-heard-blues-'til-you-heard-my-blues music. It all scared her, but the blues scared her more—made her painfully aware of things that she wanted to keep hidden.

She let her chin rest on the tip of the broom then closed her eyes. The voice was strong, and it seemed as if it was holding itself back, refraining from the violence that only it knew it was capable of. Even through the walls, she could hear its strength, its mettle. It was as if the voice had become a fist and was ready to smash through plate glass, as if the knuckles had grown thick and pliable for the oncoming onslaught. Yet it comforted her, somehow. And she didn't know if it was the silkiness that she detected underneath the melody that did it, or the reassurance that rode the bridge into the chorus...

Mrs. Lee bent down and pulled a piece of straw from the broom. She put it in her mouth and chewed. She crossed her arms across her breasts and tried to convince herself that what she was feeling about Gabriel and the man with the nice dress shoes was concern and not envy. As she walked back to the store after leaving Old Man's house, she told herself that no one but her would be able to hold Gabriel together if that man hurt him. She knew the pain that floated in the rims of his eyes and knew that only her arms could soothe him. She knew how to heal him, knew how to bring him back to the place that made him forget the weight of loneliness.

Mrs. Lee sighed. She scratched the crease in her head and let her fingers massage the tightness in her scalp. Why didn't Gabriel let her handle it? she thought. Why didn't he let her make that man leave?

The envy began, she realized, when she saw how easy it was for Gabriel to let that man into a place that he had closed up the moment Mrs. Lee found him in that box behind her store. Gabriel hesitated only slightly before he made a decision about the value of this man; all of this, she realized, he had done without her. These people, she thought to herself, these people walk thin lines and can cross them anytime that they feel, can walk on both sides and decide, without fear or consequence, which side to stay on. One day a man shows up with one letter, mentions Gabriel's father, and the two—Gabriel and the man with the nice shoes—are connected in a way that she and Gabriel would never be. And even though Gabriel wouldn't admit it, there was an ease there, a comfort between the two that startled her.

But what really ate at her was the realization that Gabriel now had a chance at the life that they both dreamed of—him out loud, her in secret. He now had the opportunity to experience what she had been promised as a young girl in New York's Chinatown: happiness. Her mother braided her hair tightly and as she sat in between her mother's thick thighs, she listened to her whisper:

Happiness is your right; it belongs to you. But as she grew older, no one came to deliver on the promises that bounced off her mother's thick thighs—words that felt like a warm embrace every time she sat down to get her hair braided.

She moved to San Francisco in hopes of finding *it* and when, in 1950, she was standing on the Golden Gate Bridge ready to end it all, she did something that seemed natural to her: she licked the orange metal. As she tasted the metal, she felt a strong yet gentle hand on her leg.

"You don't have to do this," he said. His face was flat and his eyebrows connected. "I will take care of you."

She brought her tongue back into her mouth and let him help her off the bridge and into his car. Lilly didn't know if this was the happiness that her mother had told her about but what she believed was that he cared enough to tug at her leg, to touch her gently. While she sat next to him in silence, she fingered her thighs, trying to coax the words to her ears, trying to recapture that in-between-thigh feeling.

His name was Henry Brutus. He was 5'9" and as translucent as skim milk. He had red hair, and light bounced off his flat face and settled on the bridge of his nose. He lived in a large house in Santa Rosa—ranch style—that had more rooms than she had ever known. The inside was decorated with furniture in the shape of instruments. There were end tables that looked like drums—the leather on top was thin and stretched smooth; two end chairs were shaped like the double bass, the curve of their shoulders that she knew would swallow her if she sat in them. The floors were glossy, and she could see her reflection everywhere that she walked. This unnerved her. Henry's grandfather and father made wine, and when his father died, he passed on the winery business to Henry. Henry told her of vineyards that he walked through when he couldn't sleep—the grapes like shiny heads of newborn babies, the vines like the arms of anxious mothers. He spoke lovingly the names of wine that she had never heard of: *Merlot*, *Cabernet Sauvignon*, *Pinot Noir*; their names sounded as if they would expand in her mouth if she said them over and over again, as if they would suffocate her for even trying to make them her own. Henry Brutus talked most of the time, and Lilly never was able to wrap her mind around everything that was happening to her so she sat and listened to him tell her stories about wine and about grapes that he longed to cradle.

While Henry spent the majority of his days in the vineyards, Lilly walked through the house trying hard not to see her reflection in the floor. She feared that if she looked, she would see a person she no longer knew. She feared that her face would betray her, that it would reinforce what she knew to be true—that this wasn't what her mother was talking about. To avoid looking at the floor, she decided to make a pot of rice. She looked around the kitchen and was unable to find the pot or the rice. As she stood there, her arms at her side, she felt herself unraveling—she looked down and saw the panic on her face in the shiny floors. Her body started trembling, and she felt herself about to fall. To steady herself, she picked up the broom. It felt good to have something concrete to hold, to touch. Lilly took it and began to sweep the floor, began to sweep the panic out of her face, out of her eyes. Lilly did this throughout the entire house, and by the time that Henry returned, she was calm. The entire first month of living in Santa Rosa, she rose when Henry left the house and swept until her arms hurt.

After a year, he married her, and they made love in silence. Most of the time, Lilly felt handled like the fruit in his vineyards, and before he climaxed, Henry would shove his fingers in her mouth—the tips always tasted sweet. After he was finished, he would bear his large body into hers and ask, "Did we make a baby? Did I put one there?" When it became clear that one of them was unable to make a baby, Henry asked her, "How can I carry on my father's name when you can't have kids?"

She looked at him, unsure of what to say, and lowered her eyes.

He grabbed her wrists and held them tightly. "Don't look down now. Jumping from that bridge might have been the best thing." Henry left that day and that began his nights away from her.

She lay in bed at night waiting on him to take her so that she could prove to him that she was ready and able to have a child. He rarely came, and when he did come home, he lay stiff as a board next to her in bed, praying to himself that he didn't get aroused.

When she finally got the nerve to say something to him, she talked to his back as he walked out the door. "You said that you would take care of me."

Henry Brutus stopped, and she could see a ripple in his shirt as if somewhere, a tiny gust of wind had found its way into the shirt tucked into his pants. He turned around and rubbed his chin. He stared at her, and the look on his face made her avert her eyes. When she looked back up, he was gone.

Three days later, while Lilly sat at the glass table shaped like a guitar, Henry handed her a check and said, "I will take care of you. But it won't be here."

Lilly looked at the check, then at Henry, and wondered if his hands were still soft or if they would ever bend for her again. "Where will I go?"

As she rode the bus back to New York—the check neatly folded in fours and stuffed in her bra—Lilly thought about the broom and how it was the only thing that she felt that she had some control over. Henry had stopped her from ending her life, the one real decision that she had made and one that she was ready to follow through with. Henry took that away from her, and by saving her, she realized, Henry owned and controlled her. He had all the power; she had none. He owned her space; she did not. She tugged at her braids and rolled one around her finger. As the sun dipped behind the mountains and the bus engine purred, she made the decision that no one would ever take away her power again. And the only way to do this, to ensure that it would never happen, she realized, was to own things and control the things that she owned. And she decided that she would.

She waited until she was sure that she heard only Gabriel's footsteps. Mrs. Lee went up the back steps and knocked on his door. Gabriel held the door open, and Mrs. Lee was sure that most of the makeup that he usually wore was gone. "Lady, do you know what time it is?"

"Are you leaving? Are you going with him?"

"You came up her for that?" Gabriel turned away from the door and walked back into the kitchen. An open bottle of wine sat next to a half-empty glass. Gabriel picked up the glass and swallowed what was left in one gulp. "Can we talk about this tomorrow?"

"If I come here tomorrow, you might be gone."

Gabriel looked at Mrs. Lee and sighed. "If you must always be up in mine, no, I ain't going anywhere. He is staying here."

"So that he can do you the same way that everyone else does?"

"That man ain't gon' hurt nothing, child... He kissed me." Gabriel stared into the air, a smile curved his mouth, and his cheekbones were high.

"So he is Prince Charming now? Does he know that you walk around in a dress all day?"

"Yes, he knows. He doesn't care. He told me he didn't care."

"Everyone cares, Gabriel. They all care."

"So, the real tea comes out."

"You know that I don't care. But he won't be there for you long when he realizes that they are staring at him because you are in a dress. What are you all going to do, sit in this apartment all day? Play lovey-dovey in my store?"

"Look, like I said, he don't care. He wants me for me. He told me that he has always loved me." Gabriel looked at

Mrs. Lee. "He told me that he wants to take care of me."

"Then what?"

"What do you mean? We will be together. Why is that hard for you?"

"Who's going to be around when this ends badly, Gabriel? You don't even know him."

"You don't know him."

"I know you, and that's enough. Don't let him stay. Don't let him hurt you."

"It looks like you are the one trying to hurt me, Miss Thing."

"I'm just trying to help you. You haven't lived in this world since you been here. It hasn't changed since you left Pittsburgh. Don't let him come back."

"I finally get a chance at something and you want me to throw it away because you are afraid that he's going to hurt me?"

"I'm not afraid—I know that he will."

"Of all the people in this world, I thought that you would be the happiest for me."

Mrs. Lee stood in silence and thought about the taste of orange metal. The way that it coated her tongue then, the way that it made her stomach hurt later as she sat in Henry's car—the feeling of being lost and saved at the same time... "Can't you see that I am only thinking about your happiness?"

8

Gabriel thought to himself: I remember this feeling, what love feels like. Like liquid, like light. After Thurman kissed him, he felt it as it coursed through his body, making everything that it touched — nerve, tendon, organ — thump with the recognition of light. When Thurman left, promising to come back, Gabriel stood at the closed door and waited to see if it would breathe, take in small gulps of air, like he did earlier. Love. Gabriel had not felt love since his mother let him sit in her lap and play with the clipped ends of her hair when he was a child. And when Thurman took the tail of his shirt and wiped away the colorful makeup, he felt love in each stroke. The tips of Thurman's fingers strummed out love on his cheeks, and when Thurman kissed him, Gabriel believed that his heart stopped, only to be revived by the light. Now, he wondered if Thurman would really come back, or would he realize that the man in a dress is just that — a man in a dress? Flawed and weary. Hiding his imperfections and feeling naked for the first time.

Thurman had stirred in him feelings that he had buried when he sat, crouched, in the last seat on the Greyhound bus as it made its way to Cleveland, Ohio. Stirred in him a longing for his mother—the one before the makeup, the one whose love was unfettered, not regulated... He had been longing for that mother, that feeling, since that day he stood on the front porch of his two-story home, free of makeup and a long skirt, with strands of blond hair still stuck to his head, watching his father speak to him through the crack of the door.

"You killed her. It wasn't enough that you pranced around here, but you had to do it up and down the street? She was disgusted, Gabriel, you know? Get out of here!"

His father, visibly shaking, closed the door as if there was a sleeping newborn in the house. The soft click of the lock rested in his shoulder blades and up and over his neck like a thick slab of marble. He roamed around Pittsburgh for three days and nights before he decided that he was going to leave.

On the fourth day, when he knew that his father would be busy with church duties, he snuck back into the house and packed a bag. Before he left he went into his parents' room and sat at his mother's vanity. He traced the mirror with his index finger. The picture of his mother was wedged in the corner. He pulled it down and sat it up so that it was facing him directly. "For you, Mama." He then put on the brightest red lipstick that he could find, leaned in, and kissed the mirror. An hour later, he sat in the last seat of the Greyhound clutching the picture of his mother...

Gabriel tried to shake away the tears that began to form pools on his high cheekbones—the tears that did manage to fall stained the white vanity a rust color. He grabbed the picture of his mother. "I think this is it, Mama."

"You need a haircut." Virginia stood over Chance, inspecting his bowed head. She almost reached to play in the straight, light-brown hair but changed her mind. There were never any concrete maternal feelings there. Nothing to make her smile in remembrance of something that he did when he was a baby or anything to make her feel anything deeper for the boy who scared her as much as he made her stomach hurt. Loving him was what people said she was supposed to do; liking him was something that she couldn't make herself do. He was eating, paying careful attention to the colorful round puffs that bobbed up and down in tinted milk. She shoved him with her elbow.

"Go tell Gabriel to take you to Ship's."

Chance put one last spoonful of cereal into his mouth. "I can go on my own."

"What did I say?" Virginia pulled her hair behind her ears and left the kitchen.

Chance sighed heavily, stood up, and walked out the door. He chewed as he knocked. When Gabriel didn't answer, he knocked louder and when Gabriel opened the door, he blurted out, "Mama said to take me to Ship's."

Gabriel looked at Chance. "Oh, did she?"

Chance nodded his head and swallowed hard. "I can go

alone."

"I will take you. Come inside. I need to talk to your mother."

Gabriel walked into Virginia's apartment and stood by the door. "You can't ask me yourself?"

Virginia sucked her teeth. "Come on, man. You take him all the time."

"'Come on, man'? Why you have an attitude with me? The only time we talk now is when we arguing."

"Anything new, Gabriel? Anything other than Roi?" Virginia was stretched across the couch. The soundless TV screen was filled with beachfront homes, blue-green waves, and teenagers running up and down the beach in multicolored swim trunks and bikinis.

"It's the same old thing, V. He leaves, comes back, and then leaves again. Who gets hurt? Not him. Only you. And I will leave it alone when you finally walk away from him. When is it going to be about you...about your child?"

Virginia sat up. "Are you going to take him or not?"

Gabriel walked over to the couch and stood over Virginia. "Who hurt you, girl?"

Virginia ran her fingers through her synthetic hair, grabbed a strand, and twisted it. She couldn't look at Gabriel because if she did, she wouldn't be able to control the tears that threatened. Hurt. He asked her about hurt and right then, as she twisted that strand of hair, the hurt unfolded faster than she thought possible. She twisted the hair faster, tighter. She then undid it and let it fall over her left eye. "I wanted to work on the stories; I left home in '65, and I wanted to be the first black woman on the stories. I wanted to be Lisa Hughes ever since my mother told me about her. Made me fall in love with what that white woman had. I had it in my mind that I could, you know, be her, live like her, and have men falling all over me. The thought of being my mother, of being on my knees all my life, crushed me. I didn't know when I knew, you know, that I couldn't be somebody's maid, that I was meant for something else, meant to be somebody else. But I couldn't tell her that, you know. She was so hurt when I told her I wanted to be like Lisa Hughes. I was a kid then. And when I went to Hollywood, I took my Shakespeare book with me, and when I auditioned I read the parts I had memorized. I read them because my teacher told me that all serious actors knew Shakespeare." Virginia looked at Gabriel and rested her head in her palm—she reached for another strand of hair and twirled it. "I stood in those lines and saw all those thin white women with blond, red, and brown hair, and I saw my black self—long, thin legs, nappy hair, eyes too far apart. No one talked to me, Gabriel. I was foreign to them, really. Black monkey with black, kinky hair. That's what one of the girls said about me when I was in line in front of her. I wanted to change then, make myself as white as I could—I tried bleaching my skin. I changed my hair...this hair," Virginia grabbed a fistful of hair. "This hair got me through the loneliest parts of my life."

"Oh, baby." Gabriel grabbed Virginia's hands and held them.

Virginia took her hands away and used them to pull her hair into a bun. "Well, you asked. That's what you get when you look under the bed for hurt."

"I can go on my own." Chance pleaded with Gabriel as they walked down St. Clair. Boys—shirtless, cigarette-smoking boys—lingered on the corner and as they passed, the boys laughed and spit at the ground in front of them. They sneered at Gabriel. One boy pranced on tippy-toe; another bent his wrist in exaggeration. Chance tried to walk ahead of Gabriel.

"I told your mama that I would take you." Gabriel noticed the distance growing between them as they walked and saw Chance look back at the boys. Gabriel tried hard not to look back at them—the shirtless, cigarette-smoking boys—but he couldn't stop himself. They were younger, leaner, but familiar. Reconstituted versions of Smokey and Bone, childhood bullies who ordered their lives off his fear, his clumsiness with his feet. They chased him through The Hill and Gabriel learned the hard way, after a winter of being hit with tightly packed snowballs, that not staring when they were on corners would save his life. Gabriel tore his eyes away from the boys, and as he walked, he remembered the stretched flesh over muscles that radiated restlessness that was both exhilarating and dangerous. Gabriel waved his hands at the boys. "Child, don't worry about them. And why are you walking so fast?"

Chance didn't look back. "I'm not."

Gabriel slowed for a second. He watched Chance get farther away from him and realized that he was uncomfortable walking with him. Most of their interaction had been in the store and his apartment. And if they did go somewhere together, Chance was never bothered by the slanted looks that Gabriel got or the "Damn, what's that?" that he heard when he walked past people. Gabriel drew in a long breath and then let it out slowly. He couldn't let this ruin his mood. Last night, Thurman had kissed him, had wiped away all of the thick makeup that he wore, sat him down, and looked him in the face.

"Don't wear any more makeup," Thurman said. He traced Gabriel's high cheekbones and let the tip of his finger rest on the bridge of Gabriel's nose. "This is who I want to love and take care of." And Thurman kissed him again. For the first time, someone was going to take care of him. He sighed and let Chance walk ahead of him.

Before they got to Ship's, Chance stopped abruptly and turned toward Gabriel. "Please let me go in alone."

"Go on, boy."

Chance reluctantly walked into the shop. He sat down in Ship's chair without looking him in the face.

"You a'ight, little man?"

"He is fine."

Ship looked at Gabriel and slanted his eyes. "I asked him."

Chance nodded his head slowly and then let his chin rest on his collarbone.

"Boy, pick your head up." Ship said this as he looked at Gabriel.

Gabriel looked around the shop. Two men—one with a crooked mustache, the other in blue overalls—sat at a table with checkers; another leaned against an old Pepsi machine, his finger resting on a yellowed dispenser button. Lined against the walls, across from the barber chairs, men lowered their heads and kicked at pieces of hair. On the counter were racks with bags of plain Lay's, Doritos, and barbecue pork rinds; white rags hung off sinks like overdone pasta. It seemed as if they had collectively stopped breathing, as if Gabriel had sucked in all of the air when he inhaled. Gabriel looked at Chance and saw the boy's eyes film over. He placed a ten-dollar bill into his lap and let his eyes sweep over the boy. Gabriel knew how shame gave way to fear and loathing, and as he stood in front of Chance, he saw shame planted firmly in the boy's face. "I will see you at home, Chance."

The tingling started at the tip of his toe and spread to his foot as they walked down the street and saw the boys mocking them. Chance felt the tingling and walked faster, hoping that it would go away. It spread further, up his calves, to his knees, when one of the boys—shirtless, cigarette-smoking boys—walked tiptoe up the street, swinging his hips in exaggerated movements. As Chance walked faster, he stumbled. When he caught himself, he stopped and asked Gabriel to wait outside of the barbershop. And when Gabriel refused, the tingling spread to his chest and throbbed. Chance sat in the chair and didn't raise his eyes until Gabriel was outside and up the street. While Gabriel was still in the shop, Chance curled his fist on the arms of the barber chair, the blood running from his hands making him even clearer than he was. He was old enough to walk alone and now old enough to understand that what Gabriel was wasn't what the other men wanted to see or have around them. Sitting in the chair, he lifted his head and watched the men in the barbershop, some of their faces were tight like stretched rubber, their hands with nothing to do. There were slight grimaces on some of their faces, on others, blank stares. Gabriel had interrupted something sacred, something old and private, and the way that the men disregarded him with their blank and unyielding bodies, proved it to Chance. When Gabriel finally left the shop, Chance let himself breathe and let himself feel something that he hadn't felt for Gabriel all his life: indifference.

After he was finished, Chance walked home slowly, replaying in his mind the conversation of the men.

"Can you believe that shit?" Ship said while holding the clippers. "That fag had the nerve to walk in here like he got some kids."

"Shit, man," Lil' Jay said as he leaned his body against the Pepsi machine; he held a brush like a gun. "Who walks out the house like that?" Earlier, while Gabriel was there, he was the only one who looked him in the eye. He was as tall as Gabriel—six feet, and the color of crushed graham crackers—and wasn't about to let Gabriel think that he was bothered by his presence.

Ship turned on the clippers, and they hummed—he held them like a surgeon, precise and with care. His thick shoulders, tight with frustration, bulged out of his white barber's coat. His hair was streaked with silver, his lips were pink, but his mustache was a deep, inky black. "Shit like that burns me up. Look, I don't care what you do in your bedroom, but don't walk down *my* street and into *my* shop, with all that shit on, pretending. You got a dick just like all of us."

"You see how he was looking at us?" an old man said as he sat at the checkers table. His salt-and-pepper hair was thin at the crown of his head; one hand was curved as if it had frozen around a pop can.

"Yeah, man. That was nasty."

"Don't they know it's nasty?"

"Hell naw, man. They think that shit is cute."

"It wouldn't be bad, really, if they stayed in the house. Stayed away from us, you know. Live your life in your house, and leave the *for real* living to us normal black folk."

"It got to be a law about that shit, you know? Something that says if you are a man, you have to dress like, look like, smell like, shit, *be* a man, you know. Be a man!"

"I feel sorry for their fathers...waking up every day, knowing that your son walking around in a dress. That shit would split me in half," said Lil' Jay. His face had angles — light bounced off of it, making it seem dull, gray. He continued to brush.

"He got close to you, Ship," said another man in stonewashed jeans, a black wifebeater, and cornrows.

"Get the hell out of here. That thing know better. I'm telling you, that shit ain't right, and somebody needs to kick him in his ass."

"A size 12 shoe."

"Right up his ass... I bet it wouldn't be the first thing up there."

The shop erupted in laughter, and heads nodded approvingly.

Ship turned Chance away from him and edged up the nape of his neck. "My man LeRoi said that fag is always up in his business, messing him and Virginia up. Nosey as hell. That's why he don't stick around her much. "

"Oh, yeah?"

"Yeah, what else they got to do, you know?"

"Trying to decide which dress to wear... Shit, that ain't nothing real to do."

"I heard that's all they do, be up in somebody's business...faggots."

Then all the men stopped and looked at Chance. They got quiet again and went back to what it was that they were doing before Gabriel walked into the shop.

Chance stopped at the corner of Coit and 135th on St. Clair and leaned against an abandoned bakery. He knew that he could be gone as long as he wanted because his mother wouldn't look for him. He picked up some rocks and called for an orange and white cat that meowed to him from across the street. Once the cat got closer, Chance pelted it with the rocks, and the cat darted back across the street. He tossed the last rock in his hand and pretended that he was catching a baseball. Something that he had never done before because he had no one to do it with. He didn't have anyone to tell him how to throw a slider or a curve ball, no one to tell him to snap his wrist while shooting the basketball, no one to teach him the art and science of the three-point shot. Who will teach him how to deal with the girls who roll their eyes at him, the ones who secretly break his heart? Who, he thought, would teach him how to do those things? He had never seen Gabriel in anything but a skirt or dress, so how could he? And when LeRoi was around, he only played the guitar or argued with his mother, and then left in the middle of the night. These men were only a part of his life because of his mother; they tolerated him because his mother couldn't. But he liked LeRoi the best because when he came back, the joy that his mother felt and radiated made her forget, temporarily, the hatred she had for him.

When LeRoi was around, things were good—Virginia acted like he was her son, and LeRoi didn't back away from him or make him go in his room while he polished his guitar. But when he was gone, Chance moped around with his mother, praying the same prayer that he knew that she must have said, too: bring him back, Lord, bring him back. Chance now pulled at the tufts of grass that struggled out of the cracks of concrete. He twisted the blades until they looked like parsley and let them fall like confetti. Chance never knew why LeRoi left, and when he heard that it was because of Gabriel, the tingling that spread and throbbed in his heart stopped. He couldn't understand why Gabriel would do it. Why he would make LeRoi go away. But it must have been a mistake, because how could Gabriel make someone like LeRoi leave? How could a man in a dress make a real man leave and not want to come back to his family, to his son? Chance kicked the boarded-up door multiple times until the bottoms of his feet hurt. He wanted to know why, wanted to ask Gabriel why he did it, why he sent his father away.

The little white boys on the reruns that I watch — Happy Days *and* Leave it to Beaver *— look like me. I see myself in their faces and wonder why I don't live like them, don't smile like them. I wonder why I don't play with my father in backyards like theirs, why I don't sit down and talk to my father like they do theirs after they get into trouble. I sit in front of the TV and remember not the faces of the little white boys, because they are mine, but the faces of their fathers, to see if some part of me is in them. My mother doesn't ask me if I know that I am different. It is in the way that she looks at me, the way that she doesn't touch me or tell me I love you like the Beav's mom does — her sunny hands always holding a pie or rubbing the Beav's head. She tells me that I am not like her with the way she looks at me, as if I am someone who invaded her and made himself known without her permission. I see the difference in the faces around me — colors that I don't have, thick noses and eyebrows that I don't have.*

At school, they call me Smoke — my mother doesn't know this, but how could she? — because they say that sometimes when they look at me, I disappear like smoke. It is not cool or said with affection; they say it to hurt, to scold, because they are not my friends and I am not theirs. I don't get picked for games, and the girls smile at me and roll their eyes upward at me when they think that I am not looking. I don't say much in class, and my teachers think that I am "special." They tell my mother this over the phone, and she looks at me sideways, nodding her head in agreement. And I don't know what she is agreeing to: me being special or that she has to be the one to deal with it.

If I am not watching TV, I am listening to grown-ups. Before LeRoi came, my mother and Gabriel talked a lot, and I listened. Listening to them, I learned what loneliness was. The way their voices went in and out—the soft parts so low I had to lean in to hear, the high parts making my hands tremble. The way their heads would lower at the mention of a name—Carl, Junior, Walter, James—the way that their lips formed around those names and released them slowly, told me that the loneliness came from those men, was made more permanent by them. I learned that loneliness was only for the person who was left with it…

Gabriel told me I was too grown when I told him that I was lonely. He said to me, "Why are you lonely? You are a kid. Go play with other kids, and stay out of grown folks' business." I just looked at him and went to turn on the TV. Lonely didn't have an age, I wanted to tell him. Lonely happened every day I went to school and was shut out of the basketball and flag-football games; lonely happened every day the girls rolled their eyes at me. Every time they called me Smoke, made "poof, poof" noises with their mouths…

When LeRoi came, I didn't feel lonely anymore. I didn't feel left out. He let me watch him play. He didn't call me Smoke or look at me sideways because I had clear skin and funny colored eyes. He even showed me how to play his guitar once. Let me sit in his lap and hold the guitar while he guided my hands.

"Like this, man. Hold her real gentle. You have to be gentle with her."

I smiled real hard and did everything that he told me.

154 | The Butterfly Lady

"Okay, okay, that was good. But you can't be that rough, man. Next time we can practice some more, okay?"

I bopped my head up and down and sat in the corner thinking that this is what fathers do. They help take the lonely away. And when he stopped coming that first time, I stood on the porch watching for him. Waiting for him to show me the rest, what he promised he would do... I waited for a week, and when he came back, I almost jumped in his lap. "Whoa, man. Give me a second." I backed away and watched him sit on the couch. My mother stood in the kitchen doorway with her hands on her hips, never taking her eyes off of him. "Chance, go in your room...and close the door." I went and lay on the floor with my ear to the ground and listened. I knew she missed him, too, because of the way that his name rolled off of her lips.

After that, he stayed for longer days and stayed away even longer. I would look for him then, go to the places where my mother told people on the phone that his "triflin' ass" would be. I watched Portia to see if he would show up and be with her; he wasn't coming back, and I didn't want Gabriel to take me to get a haircut—I wanted to do it on my own. He didn't see that I wanted a father—not someone playing one. The boys on the corner made my toes tingle. It felt like when I stuck my tongue on a nine-volt battery. And as we walked and as they got closer, it tingled. They walked like him, their lips stuck out, bouncing around like he did. I saw them even as I walked faster, felt them behind us, making fun of us. I hated the tingling—it made me dizzy, made me embarrassed, made me hate Gabriel for wearing a dress... I was trying to walk faster, but they followed, he followed; he was always there, Gabriel. Even when LeRoi wasn't. He was there, one arm wrapped around my mother, the *other hanging off his hip, his arm shaped like someone was going to shoot an arrow from it. I didn't want Gabriel to comfort my mother. I wanted LeRoi. I wanted him to sit me on his lap, teach me how to play that guitar. He had to come back, he had to, and when he does, I will be ready. And when he does, he will look at me and not turn his head, not care that my skin is clear.*

"Virginia?" Gabriel knocked on the door before he turned the knob and let himself in. The sun was starting to set, and the warm stickiness of July clung to him. He hadn't seen Chance and wanted to see if he had missed him. Gabriel walked into the apartment, and Virginia's bedroom door was open; she was lying in her bed. He walked into the room and sat in the chair directly across from her. "Have you seen Chance?"

Virginia didn't answer at first. She stared out of the small window where a small plant sat in the windowsill. "I thought he was with you."

Gabriel thought back to the shame and fear he both felt and saw in Chance and turned his head. "You know I can't be sitting around holding no almost-grown man's hand. I told him to come home when he was finished." Gabriel reached over and smoothed out the covers. It was hot in the room, and Gabriel wondered why the heat hadn't swallowed her yet. He walked over to the window and cracked it slightly; slips of wind blew into the room. He stuck his finger in the flowerpot—bone dry. He told himself to water it before he left.

"He used to sing to me right outside of that window," she said, her voice dry and laborious. "Sang to me all night, one time."

"I know, honey. I was the one who called the police on him, remember?" Gabriel laughed and picked up the pot. "I'm going to water this plant." He lifted it so that Virginia could see.

"You are always good to me. Good to Chance, Gabriel." Virginia stretched her arms then crossed them like she was about to be lowered in a casket.

Gabriel watched her do this, walked out the room, went to the kitchen, and ran water in the pot. As he walked back to the bedroom, Gabriel heard a knock at the door. He opened it, and LeRoi stood in front of him.

"Where is Virginia?" LeRoi tried to push his way past Gabriel.

"She's not here, and she don't want you here."

"Move out my way, faggot."

Gabriel planted himself in the doorway. "You ain't coming in here disrupting her life."

"Who the fuck are you?" LeRoi was screaming now, and the veins in his forehead throbbed.

"Go on, LeRoi. Don't nobody want your raggedy ass."

"Move out of my way, Gabriel."

He was in Gabriel's face now, and Gabriel could see the beauty in this man, could see why she loved him so much; his freckles moved with his heartbeat. "Baby, you ain't had a fight until you had one with me."

"LeRoi?" Virginia stood behind Gabriel. "LeRoi?"

"Go back to bed, Virginia. Let me take care of this."

"Move, Gabriel."

Slowly, Gabriel moved his body to one side of the door

and folded his arms.

"She said move, punk!" LeRoi shouted.

"I ain't going nowhere, baby."

LeRoi lunged towards Gabriel, but Virginia put her palms on his chest to stop him. "What you want, Roi? What you got to say this time?"

"Baby, I'm back. I put it down."

"Back for what, Roi?"

"For you."

"Is that what you told Portia? Is that why she tried to kill me?"

He put his arm around Virginia's waist but she pushed it away. "I don't know what you talking about, baby. But I'm here."

Virginia shook her head and pushed him further away. "I *been* waiting on you for a long time, Roi...a long time."

"Look, I'm done. You see?" He showed her his hands, the lines in his palm dark against the light flesh. "I put Ruth down. I put her down for you." He walked toward Virginia, and she backed away. "Let me love you, V. Let me love you back to me."

Virginia walked back to her bedroom.

LeRoi would have left and walked away quietly if Gabriel wasn't there watching him beg her to take him back. LeRoi had given up his guitar, had given up playing for his mother, for Virginia, and Gabriel stood there with his lips pursed, his hands folded across his chest in disappointment, and watched him lose his manhood to a woman who now threw him away. He should have left, but he couldn't after that, could he? He yelled, "How you gon' leave me? Huh? I give it all up for you, and you gon' walk away from me?" LeRoi charged through the door and pushed past Gabriel. In two strides, he had Virginia by her elbow and jerked her around so that she was facing him.

"Let me go, Roi."

"You can't leave me, again…not again." The sound of clicking heels filled his ears, and he shook her as hard as he could. He threw Virginia across the room, and she landed with a thud. "You left me once. I waited for you. I pissed myself waiting for you." LeRoi stood over her and cocked his fist. Before he could hit her, Gabriel tackled him to the ground. They rolled around the room, and when Gabriel was on top of LeRoi, he started beating him in the face.

Virginia stood up and screamed. "Gabriel, get off of him! Leave him alone!"

Gabriel pushed Virginia back.

Her screams grew louder and she pounded on Gabriel's back. "I hate you, Gabriel! Leave him alone. Leave. *My*. Man. Alone!"

Gabriel stopped with his fist in midair and looked back at Virginia, the hair in her face made her look savage, and a lump formed in his throat. Gabriel got up slowly and backed into the wall.

LeRoi wiped the blood from his nose with the back of his hand. He pointed to Virginia. "You let him do this to me!" LeRoi spit the blood that had accumulated in his mouth at Gabriel's feet and walked out of the apartment.

Gabriel patted his head. His wig was on the floor, and he reached for it but stopped. He felt the breeze from the window on his legs; his skirt was ripped, and his blouse had spots of blood the size of quarters on it. Virginia looked at the open door and turned back to Gabriel. Both breathing heavily, they stared at each other. He was gone; she was gone. He couldn't breathe anymore; she couldn't breathe anymore. And it was all his fault, he thought: never knowing when to leave it alone, let the hurt stay under the bed. Virginia looked back at the door and the tears that flowed steadily suddenly stopped. She walked to her bedroom and closed the door. Gabriel stood against the wall, patting his head and trying to catch his breath.

Gabriel picked up his wig, put it back on his head, and adjusted it. He looked down at his hands, and there was dried blood on his knuckles. He rubbed his hands together—he suddenly was cold and tried to hold together the largest rip in his skirt. Gabriel walked slowly to the door, and before he walked out, he looked back at the spot where she stood: the savagery that he saw—hair all over her head, quivering lips, eyes poking out of her head—was not for LeRoi, but for him. What Gabriel finally knew when he looked into her face, into the deepness of her eyes, into the roving hunger, was that she would, if she could, tear him piece by piece to save LeRoi, if she could. What he also knew was that no matter what he did for Virginia, no matter how much he was there for her and Chance, that she would never be satisfied. Would never truly appreciate him or what he had done for her all of these years. Virginia's love and affection, like his parents', was conditional— contingent on the mood and the whim of her beating heart.

Her love for him was never meant to heal; it was a means of getting over on him, a way to muscle him aside whenever she felt like it. Gabriel's eyes swept over the spot where she stood, which was empty and full at the same time. He now knew what hurt looked like when you poked your head under the bed.

It was Old Man who told Chance that LeRoi was back. "What you doing out here, boy? Where is your mama?"

"I'm on my way home."

"Well, hurry up and get there." Old Man stood there until Chance started to move.

"Yes, sir." Chance placed his hands in his back pants pocket.

"Oh, and LeRoi should be at your mama's."

Chance no longer felt the throbbing in his chest. LeRoi had come back because he promised. He had come back to teach him, to be his father, and Chance knew that if he learned fast, if he learned how to not hurt the strings, then LeRoi would stay this time. At the thought of LeRoi staying permanently, Chance ran faster. And when he got to his door, LeRoi busted out of it and knocked him down to the ground. Chance looked at LeRoi's face and saw the dry blood around his nose and the swollen top lip. His shirt had streaks of blood and was untucked. Before Chance could say, "I knew you were coming back," LeRoi picked him up by the collar and twisted his shirt so that Chance was close enough to feel the heat of his breath. "You think I'm shit, too?" Chance flinched as spit hit his skin. LeRoi pulled him closer. "I gave up my music for her, and she picked him over me." He let Chance go, stuffed his shirt back into his pants, and walked away.

Chance sat with his back to his door. He bounced a yellow tennis ball against the wall. The *thump, thump, thump* was louder and heavier than his breathing. In his lap rested a sharp kitchen knife. Earlier, he picked up the broken lamp, moved the couch back to its original place, organized the scattered newspapers, and made sure that his mother was in the bed. Now, he let the ball hit the ground; it bounced down the steps. He then ran his index finger along the blade; a thin layer of blood coated his finger. He stood up and placed the knife in his back pocket. He walked into Gabriel's apartment. It was dark except for the light from the vanity—Gabriel's shadow was cast against the wall. Chance walked in and turned on the TV. *Happy Days* was on—Richie was asking the Fonz for dating advice…

"Chance?" Gabriel was seated at the vanity, his hand resting on a glass.

Chance stood behind him.

"You want something? How is your mama?"

Chance didn't answer. He put his hand in his back pocket and grabbed the handle of the knife.

"Boy, did you hear me?"

"Why are you always around? Why did you make him go away?"

Gabriel rubbed his forehead then took a drink from the

glass. "What I tell you about grown folks' business?"

Gabriel looked at Chance through the mirror. "You have plenty of time to be grown. And trust me, it ain't all that glamorous." Gabriel laughed and looked at his mother, her smile never wavering. "How is your mama?" Gabriel said as he looked into Chance's eyes. "I didn't mean to. I can't get it right with her..." Gabriel stopped himself and stroked the lip of the glass. He couldn't look Chance in the eye, and so he stared toward a corner of the room. "Go home. I will see you tomorrow. I'm tired."

Chance thought he heard the soft strumming of a guitar. He cocked his head toward the window. Did he come back? Did he realize that he was wanted, needed? He listened harder, and heard, he was sure, the soft moan of someone in pain. Of someone who needed to be found.

With one motion, he slit Gabriel's throat.

If Mrs. Lee stuck her tongue out, she could capture the tears. Earlier, Virginia called her and all that she could make out was "Gabriel...throat...open...dead..." Now, she stood outside his door, her arms stretched across the doorway like a barrier, waiting on the people to take him away. She tried to stop her body from shaking, from giving up on her. She couldn't let her arms down, couldn't let anyone else in to hurt Gabriel. He had come to her, those many years ago, and it was her responsibility to make him safe, to make him better. She told him to leave that little boy alone, told him to let them be. Him and his mother. Her body shook harder; the tips of her fingers were numb from holding the outline of the door. Eventually, she let her arms down and slid to the floor. She had let him down, she thought. She hadn't loved him enough. But how could she when he wouldn't listen to her, wouldn't let anyone too close? He was in there, throat cut from ear to ear. The people who killed Gabriel, she let them in. And they took him away from her.

Old Man walked into Ship's Barbershop, and the chatter he heard before ceased. The men eyed him and folded their hands. Old Man sighed and asked Ship if he had seen LeRoi. Without looking into Old Man's eyes, Ship shook his head, no. These past few days had been heavy for everyone, even if they didn't like Gabriel. The murder of someone who you despised was one thing; knowing personally the hands that did the killing soured everyone's stomach. That night, Old Man stood behind all of the folks who stood outside Lee's to watch them roll out the body. Sometimes, he wished that he had more courage, more strength to weep openly for Gabriel, to fight for Gabriel. But he didn't. And Old Man didn't know if he would ever weep again. Eunice's leaving rattled a part of him that he thought he had solved; now, her child, the only thing Old Man had left of Eunice, was nowhere to be found. And what was even more perplexing was that LeRoi's guitar sat in its case, leaned against the right arm of the couch.

The day that he went back, LeRoi tried to tell Virginia what he had learned. As he walked up the stairs, he replayed in his mind the moment he realized that it was the guitar that kept the heels coming, kept them alive in his head. It had taken over his life, the clicking heels, and he wondered what his mother would do if he found her. What she would say when he handed the guitar to her and explained that it kept her connected to him. That it was the only reason that he roamed, to try and keep up with the clicking heels, that he followed the music hoping that it lea to her, hoping that he could finally rest. He wanted to tell Virginia that if he stayed, and that if she let him, he could bury the heels, clip them, and stick them away for good. He told himself this as he took each step—that Ruth, his guitar—kept his mother around even when she didn't want to be around. Made her visible even when she was invisible... LeRoi had to do it, had to put the music down to live, you see...and he had planned to tell Virginia that, planned to let her put his fingers in her mouth to stop him from searching, stop him from playing his mother back into existence.

When she realized that she would never see LeRoi again, Virginia spit out the note and tried to pat it dry. It was too late; the words had been destroyed. But she remembered them and mumbled as she paced back and forth in her apartment. Her child had killed the one person who cared about him more than she did. And she let it happen. Virginia could not watch them take Gabriel's body away, so she climbed into her tub and stroked her honey-blond hair. For three days, Virginia tried to let it out—the gut-wrenching scream that she heard in her head every day since she saw the neck that looked like the open flap of an envelope. But it stayed stuck like a lump of coal, settled in her stomach. She hadn't cried for anyone other than herself in a long time, and her body stubbornly agreed. She wanted to call out her child's name, "Chance," but the only thing she was able to get out was, "Roi?"

And God knows LeRoi was the last person that she should have been calling for. Gabriel had been right, had always been right when it came to her heart. Gabriel knew her, loved her, and if she didn't resent him so much for it, then maybe, just maybe, she would have treated him better. Virginia turned her face to the other side of the tub's lip; it was cooler. She was still fully dressed and could smell herself. She laughed out loud. "Gabriel would walk in here, look at me crazy, and politely turn on the shower and not even worry about my hair, bitch..." The laughter was the first sound she heard from herself since she locked herself in her bathroom. When she stopped laughing, Virginia thought about her mother, and for the first time, really, she wondered what her mother must have felt when she found Virginia holding the picture of that white woman. "Oh, Mama, I didn't want to be her, and I didn't love her more than you. I loved the thrill, the way that white woman lived her life freely. You were never free, mama, never free, and if I stayed, I wouldn't have been free either."

On the fourth day, Virginia gave up and let the pain swallow her.

The letter was still in the paper arms of the Bible. Thurman sat on the edge of the hotel bed, and stared at the blazer that hung off the chair like a prostitute. Although he didn't know what was in the letter, he had memorized the handwriting of Deacon Smith and the slight fold in the left-hand corner of the envelope. Slightly worn and faded, Thurman knew that the envelope had sat with the Deacon for some time. If only he had done what he promised to do: give the letter to Gabriel and come back to Pittsburgh... That was what he swore that he would do, and he knew that somehow, the Deacon's life had become inextricably tied to his, and he figured that that was the way that it was supposed to be. The Deacon had come to rely on him heavily, had even shouldered as much of Thurman's burden as he had, but Thurman didn't hesitate to let that heaviness go when he saw Gabriel look up at him. Thurman reached for the Bible in the drawer but stopped. He knew that there wasn't time, really. No time to tell a son that the father was dying, no time to tell the father that the son he wanted couldn't be anything other than what he was, no time to tell a son that the father didn't really want him to come home — only wanted him to know about the death he feels the son caused.

Thurman didn't mean to fall back in love with Gabriel. That was something from his teen years, something he tucked away from himself. Never believing in the possibility, fearful of the actualization. When he left Gabriel that day, he decided as he waited on the Number 1 bus that going back to Pittsburgh was not the answer — his place was with Gabriel. And as he packed the little brown suitcase that held a toothbrush, two pairs of cotton briefs, two white shirts, and a brown suit, he decided to call Deacon Smith and tell him that he couldn't find Gabriel.

But Gabriel was dead now, and Thurman didn't know what hurt more: seeing the slender wrist plunged into darkness or not delivering the letter that he left sitting in the Bible.

Thurman picked up the phone and dialed the Deacon's number. It rang three times, and right when he was about to hang up, he heard a raspy "Hello" on the other end. Thurman held the receiver tight against his ear, the sound of sickness agonizing. "I couldn't find him, Deacon. I'm coming home."

Each time Chance stopped in the places where he thought LeRoi might be—in the Low Down where he saw Portia, whose eyes looked wet even though she was smiling, or at Ship's Barbershop, where two old men played checkers with toothpicks sticking out the corners of their mouths—he tried to rub the blood off of his hands. He had been trying for days, but the blood coated his palms, making them the color of dried roses. His feet hurt, and he was tired of hiding and sleeping in dark alleyways. Chance wanted his mother but knew that she would be no good, would be of no use to him. Chance had to bring LeRoi back, had to find the music and let LeRoi know that he didn't look at him differently, that he didn't think that he was shit, too. Chance roamed the streets knowing that if he found the music, then he would find him, too...but the music was gone. It had lost its home, lost its means of survival. No more spaces to create and then fit into. No more throats to crawl up; no more lips to pour out of.

So what does it do? Who does it reach for when the

guitar man has lost his way, has given in to the helplessness that he tried to play away? How does it go on when the always-dreaming lady stuffs notes back into her aching throat, stuffs misery back into a place that can barely hold what is already there? What does it do when the music it hears itself, the music that it wants to be like, sound like, feel like, abandons it as well? The music is living and breathing, and it requires the living and breathing to make it what it is. To make it move, form, and shape itself around itself. It can no longer dip in and out of the lining of the heart's walls, no longer splinter into pieces inside the lungs. The music is lost like they all are now—it no longer loves. The music has given in, given up. The music is gone, gone, gone.

Acknowledgements

I would like to thank T.A. Noonan for taking a chance on this book. I am grateful to her and the folks at Flaming Giblet and Sundress for their help and care with my work. Also, I wanted to write individual things about a lot of folks, but words — and space — can't fully express what you all mean to me. Please accept my listing of you all as my eternal gratitude.

My mentees: Keith, Tony, Murad, Harrison, Nikeeta, Kijafa, D'andre, Jeremy, Gerald, Haskel, Trerod, Randryia, Hannah, Leonard, Jason, and Covasky.

My Brothers in the Bond: Issam, Derrick, Mark, Diallo, Eddie, Jelani, Cobb, Fon, Mike D., Shaun, She'Ron, Decatur, Kendrick, Travis, Carl, Mo, and Thurman.

My best friends: Gaurin, Sye, Scott, David G.C., Brian G., Dwayne, Jason Eason, and Rachel.

The ladies: Deauna, Roslynn, Yalonda, Terra, Juanita, Jada, Kamille, Dr. P. Deroze, Nichelle, Vivian, Diane, Avery, and LaShanda.

The ones who inspire me: Aunt Ann, Rhonda, Dr. John Roberts, Dr. Walton Muyumba, Dr. Britta Coleman, Dr. Leonard Slade, John High, Anton, Dana Johnson, Mrs. Crockrom, Walter Lundy, L. Lamar, and Charlton.

My Florida crew: Darlene, Ana, Scott, Thomas Tucker (ha, ha), and Jonathan Lang.

The artists: Marc B., thank you for the dope photos; Stevie, thank you for the great cover art and the friendship.

The ones who keep me sane and motivated: Wendy, Jalin, and Jevon.

Last but not least, I want to thank the one who inspired me to pick up a book and read, my mother—I thank God for the time that we had together and for the gift that you helped nurture!

About the Author

photo by Marc Brutus

Danny M. Hoey, Jr., an Ohio native, has stories published in *WarpLand*, *Women in REDzine*, *Mandala*, *African Voices Magazine*, and *SNReview*. *The Butterfly Lady* is his first novel.

CPSIA information can be obtained
at www.ICGtesting.com
Printed in the USA
FSOW02n0639281016